Loving You

A Small Town Second Chance Romance

Book 2

Connor Brothers series

By Leah J. Busboom

D1527693

Dedication

To all of you who enjoy reading a delightful, romantic story just like me!

To the kind and caring people of Minnesota where I lived for 15 years. You inspired this story.

To my amazing husband—I couldn't do this without your love and support.

Table of Contents

I can't figure out the mathematics of this, I just know I love you.

Graham (Jude Law), *The Holiday*

Chapter One

Max

My footsteps echo in the empty hallway, sounding overly loud even to my ears. Summer school is in session so there aren't as many students as during the regular semester. Not much has changed in five years. Same drab gray paint and worn linoleum. The building could really use some sprucing up. Maybe Connor Construction could bid to renovate the place—though with limited academic budgets I know that's a pipe dream.

As I round the corner, I see the light on in Professor Maddie's office, if that's still her same office. I remember spending hours getting math tutoring and drooling over the professor. I hope she didn't know the extent of my secret crush on her. I thought at the time that she might have felt it too, but her loyalty and devotion to her husband drove me away. She was happily married. Period.

Then Mom showed me the newspaper article about Maddie's husband's tragic death. He died just over two years ago, but the wrongful death lawsuit took forever to settle and eventually made front page news. To say that information rocked my world is an understatement.

Jack Henderson was killed while I was still living in Wisconsin, where I'd fled to finish my degree and nurse my unrequited lovesick heart. When I returned home to run the family construction business, it never occurred to me to look up happily married Professor Maddie. Now there's nothing standing in my way of pursuing a relationship. Here I am, ready to bravely lay my cards on the table and see if the chemistry I felt is still there.

Time may heal all wounds, but the hole in my heart for Maddie never healed. During the past five years, I was never ready to let go of the possibility of *her*. That's why I'm here, sweating through my shirt, with my heart thumping in my chest.

My footsteps slow as I approach the open doorway, light spilling out into the hallway. A brass plate beside the door reads: *Professor Madeleine Henderson, Mathematics*. The anticipation of seeing her again is equal parts dread and anticipation, not knowing how she will react to seeing me again. I wipe my sweaty palms on my blue jeans, plaster a smile on my face, then knock on the doorframe. I take a step forward and gaze at the love of my life.

She looks up from the computer screen, a pair of glasses perched on her cute nose. My heart skips a beat or two as my eyes roam over her. Five years has only made her more beautiful. Her long brunette hair cascades down her back, not in the usual bun or ponytail I was accustomed to. A smile spreads across her face as I walk closer to her desk.

"Maxwell Connor? What are you doing here?" A tinge of excitement and trepidation leaks through her words. *Is she happy to see me or not?*

My unsteady legs no longer want to hold me upright, so I plop into the chair across from her desk. She raises an eyebrow when it takes me several seconds to respond. Scrubbing the stubble on my cheek, I plunge ahead. "I heard about your husband's tragic accident." The words blurt from my mouth as if days of practicing what to say taught me nothing. The smile on her face slips a little, so I continue, hoping to repair any damage my blunt words caused. "Maddie, I'm sorry. That's not how I wanted this conversation to start."

She nods. Although her expression remains closed off, I see tears filling her beautiful brown eyes.

"I didn't know about . . . about all that until I saw that article in the newspaper. And it's taken me this long to get the courage to come see you. Because I want you to know how sorry I am, and how much I want us to be friends. And maybe something more . . ."

My breath swooshes out along with my words, as if I can't say them fast enough. *Man, am I ever bungling this.*

The expression on her face stays neutral, but the look in her eyes tells me she isn't immune to me either. "Are you back living in Connor's Grove?"

She avoids the main topic of a relationship with me like someone would avoid poison ivy.

Clearing my throat, I reply, "Yes, I came back about a year ago when my uncle had a heart attack. I'm running the family construction company now and I plan to stay here."

Her eyes widen, but she remains silent.

I'm doing all the heavy lifting here, so I hit the ball back in her court. "I've thought of you constantly for five years. Even if you're not ready to pursue a relationship with me, I'm ready to pursue one with you. I need to explore if the chemistry and feelings I had for you five years ago are still there, lying dormant. I want to take you out, get to know you again. For now, I'll take friendship if that's all you want to offer." I shrug and let the silence hang between us, waiting for her response.

She licks her lips and pushes the glasses up on her nose. "You still have a crush on me? I'm older than you. I'm your former teacher. And I'm not all that interesting."

I smile. "Maddie, I've had a crush on you since that first day in your Calculus 101 class. Surely you could tell?"

She shrugs as if all her students have a crush on her. *Maybe they do.*

I press on. "You're only five years older than me. I love the fact that you're my former mathematics professor. And I find you very interesting."

She sighs. "You always were persistent. I remember how you and Hannah always battled it out for highest grade." A small smile lights up her face.

I also smile at the memory. "How about we go with friendship first? Let's get to know each other again. I promise I'm no longer the immature guy from Calc 101."

Maddie laughs. "You weren't immature, just young and enthusiastic. I like that about you." A blush spreads across her face, telling me she might feel the chemistry too.

"Let's start with coffee or lunch. Tomorrow."

"I don't know if I'm ready to date *anyone* yet . . ." Her words trail off; sadness crosses her face, and she looks down at her hands clenched on top the desk.

I lean forward. "Hey, look at me. Just friendship for now. Lunch is a place to start—plus, you have to eat."

Her brown eyes meet my blue ones. "You won't let me say 'No,' will you?"

I shake my head.

"I'm teaching Calc 101 Wednesday from ten to noon. We can go for lunch after class."

I want to leap across the desk and kiss her, but that would be a terrible move at this point. Instead, I stand, squeeze her hand, and say, "Which classroom?"

She smiles. "Nothing ever changes around here. The same classroom when you were in the class."

Nodding, I reply, "I'm looking forward to it. I'll be here at noon on Wednesday."

As I walk back towards the hallway, I pause and glance back over my shoulder. She's smiling. Friendship is definitely on the table. Now to convince her to take things a step further. *I love a challenge.*

Chapter Two

Maddie

My heart finally stops its erratic beating once Max disappears. I take several minutes to collect myself after the bombshell he dropped at my feet. When he was my student, I knew he was attracted to me. And who wouldn't be drawn to Max's raw masculinity? But I was happily married. Jack was a wonderful husband and I was committed to him. Max Connor was just another one of my students.

But he has matured nicely, to say the least. He's more muscular, and his five o'clock shadow enhances his rugged looks and gorgeous face. But it's his brilliant smile and sharp mind that draw me to him, just like when he was my student. He soaks up information like a sponge; his zest for learning emulates my own. Don't let the sexy package fool you—Max is one intelligent man.

I wipe my sweaty palms on my pants. *What have I just agreed to?*

It's been over two years since Jack's death imploded my world. I woke up one day a happily married woman and the next minute I was a widow. He went to work just like any other day. We kissed at the door and I reminded him to pick up a gallon of milk on his way home. Since I didn't have any classes that day, I puttered around the house doing mundane tasks like laundry, cleaning bathrooms, and fixing Jack's favorite meal for dinner. The smell of cooking lasagna will now always be associated with the knock on the door that changed my life forever.

Knock! Knock!

The noise echoes the sound from years ago and pulls me from my sad musings.

"A penny for your thoughts," Professor William Bolton says as he strolls into my office. "You look like you're solving a differential equation in your head."

I resist the urge to raise my eyebrows at him as I can and routinely do solve differential equations in my head. My coworker is not the best at communicating with people. "Hello William." The guy insists on being called William, even by his closest friends. Never Bill or even Will. And he isn't hesitant to correct anyone who uses the less formal address. I'm almost surprised he doesn't insist I call him Professor Bolton. I motion to the chair on the other side of the desk, although he's already halfway sitting in it. He sits down, crosses his legs at the ankle, and stares at me. I take a few seconds to mentally compare him to Max Connor.

William is much lankier than Max, somewhat gangly in his frame. All angles and sharp corners, where Max is all strength and hardness. The professor's sandy blond hair is always mussed as if he just ran his fingers through it. He's clean shaven, and a pair of wire-rimmed glasses rest on his beak of a nose. Very scholarly looking. My pulse doesn't immediately skyrocket and my breathing remains normal when he's around.

He's been a good friend the last few years, and he's hinted several times that he wants to take things to a new level when I'm ready. William stops by my office at least once a day to chat or discuss one of our mutual students. He teaches Calc 201, so most of my students become his students at some point.

Realizing that the silence stretching between us is becoming awkward, I clear my throat. "A former student just stopped by. He caught me a bit off guard."

The professor sits up taller in his chair. "Max Connor? I passed him in the hallway on his way out."

"You know him?" I've already said too much; William looks like I just waved a red flag in front of his face. I can almost see the breath snorting out his nostrils.

"Everyone knows the Connors. His sister-in-law is taking a few classes and my good friend Professor Carrigan is her advisor. What did he want?"

I squirm in my chair. William is a good friend, but that's exactly where I think I want him to remain. A friend. On the other hand, my interest in Max Connor is much more complex. "We were just catching up. He didn't know Jack had passed away until he saw the recent article in the newspaper . . ." Pausing, I blink the moisture from my eyes, my emotions still raw whenever I talk about Jack. "Max came to express his sympathies." *And ask me out to lunch.* I clamp my lips shut, lest I share any more tidbits about the purpose of Max's visit.

William pushes his glasses up his long nose, staring at me directly through his thick lenses. I feel like I'm being cross-examined and any minute the pressure will get to me and I'll spout out, *Okay, I admit, I'm interested in Max Connor!* Instead I change the subject. Avoidance is my first instinct when faced with something I don't want to deal with head on. And I don't want to examine my feelings too closely yet. "How's Andrew Billings doing in Calc 201 this summer? You know he struggled with 101."

William chuckles. "How about we go to lunch and forget about our students? I'm starving." A smirk crosses his face as if he knows about my upcoming lunch date with Max. "And when are you going to agree to go out to dinner with me?" Apparently, William can be as persistent in his pursuit of a relationship as Max, just a bit more subtle.

My mouth falls open. We've gone to lunch hundreds of times since Jack's death, yet I've always balked at anything resembling a date, dreaming up flimsy excuses that thus far he's accepted with grace. His point blank question takes me by surprise.

I ignore the dinner comment, stand, place my computer glasses on the desk, and grab my purse from the drawer. "A quick bite at the student union sounds good. I have a class in an hour."

William's eyes bore into me for a moment as if he's going to force the dinner issue. When my stomach growls loudly, he chuckles instead and lets the question slide.

My mind spins, still comparing the two men. William's presence is comfortable—like a well-broken-in leather chair—where Max's presence pushes me out of my comfort zone, filling my head with the jangle of warning bells.

Comfortable is safe. Comfortable is good. Can I convince my heart of that?

Chapter Three

Max

The smile on my face won't go away. I have a date with Professor Maddie! Sure, it's just lunch for now, but that's a big step forward. Even though I soft peddled it as friendship, I plan on wooing the lovely professor until we're officially dating.

My eyes drift to the piles of paper on my desk, all needing my immediate attention. I better quit daydreaming about the professor and get to work.

"Matchmaker" from *Fiddler on the Roof* starts playing on my cell phone. I grab the phone as it dances across my desk with Mom's smiling face filling the screen. Knowing she'll just keep calling if I don't pick up, I swipe and answer in my most pleasant voice. "Mom, what can I do for you?"

She snorts on the other end. "Maxwell, I'm just calling to chat!"

That's highly unlikely, but I roll with it. "Okay, what did you want to chat about?"

There's a several second pause at the other end. I cringe, knowing what's coming next. "Delores Goodnight just called. Her daughter Alicia is in town for a few days . . ."

I cut this conversation off at the knees. "Mom, I'm not going on another blind date with a daughter of one of your friends."

She sighs. "But Max, Alicia is such a nice girl. She's the one who graduated from Stanford last spring. I think you two would hit it off."

Mom's uncontrollable matchmaking has become a real thorn in my side. "Do I need to remind you of the last two blind dates you set me up on? Let's see . . . Constance Anderson barely said ten words during our entire date. I thought she was going to faint at my feet when I picked her up."

Mom laughs. "You are an imposing figure, Max. But she would've gotten used to your male charm eventually."

It's my turn to snort. "Dream on, Mom. When she asked me if I'd loved reading *Pride and Prejudice* or any of Jane Austen's novels, I knew that we were as incompatible as fire and ice." *She's the ice*.

"Didn't you read *Pride and Prejudice* in high school?"

I sigh. "Mom, that's not the point."

Clearing her throat, Mom replies, "Maybe I miscalculated about Constance. But you have to admit Trudi Hudson's daughter had the potential to be an excellent match."

I roll my eyes. "Mary Beth and I also had nothing in common—"

This time Mom cuts in. "She's a big sports fan and loves pizza!"

I should have videoed our date because Mom has a very short memory span. "Right. Her idea of a good time was going to Johnson's Pub and drinking beer. She challenged every guy there to play her in billiards or foosball. I felt like a third wheel the whole time. Do you know what she said to me at the end of the evening?"

"No, what?" Mom says in a small voice.

"She said, and I quote, 'Max, I can drink you under the table. I want a man who can keep up with me. I don't see us working out long term.' She then slapped me on the back and belched louder than any guy I've ever heard. I sped out of her driveway so fast my tires squealed."

Silence greets me. I watch the clock and time Mom's comeback. A full thirty seconds later she replies, "Okay, I admit those dates didn't go so well. But I have a great feeling about Delores's daughter."

There's only one way to nip Mom's meddling in the bud. Even though I cringe to think of how she's going to blow things out of proportion, this is the only way I can get her from trying to pair me with every available daughter of her friends. "I went to see Professor Maddie yesterday."

I envision Mom's ears pricking forward like a Terrier on the hunt. "Oh? How is she?"

Keeping the chuckle to myself, I reply, "We're having lunch tomorrow. I'm hoping that's just the first date of many to come."

A loud squeal pierces my ear. I may never have full hearing in that ear again.

"Max that's wonderful! Dating a math professor will keep you on your toes. Better get the old textbooks out for a refresher." Nervous laughter from the other end of the line tells me that Mom may be the one who's bowled over by Maddie's career.

"Ha ha, Mom. Very funny," I say while suppressing a groan.

"Well, we're having a family dinner on Sunday, please invite her to come! I'd love to meet her."

No. Way. Alarm bells ring in my head. Meeting all the Connors at once is a guaranteed way to scare Maddie off. "Let's see how the first date goes before you're planning our wedding," I say with a little too much snark in my voice.

"Yes, dear. Well, she's always welcome whenever you want to invite her. Can you remind Hailey that she's supposed to bring snickerdoodles on Sunday? Your dad just loves those, and Hailey's are the best."

Dad can really pack away Hailey's snickerdoodles. Come to think of it, Dad can pack away almost any food item other than Ash's healthy salads. "Sure Mom, I'll remind her."

"I'll be waiting to hear how your lunch with the professor goes tomorrow. Bye!"

I sit for a few minutes decompressing from the call with Mom. Finally, I get up and wander into the front office where my sweet sister-in-law is glued to the QuickBooks app on her computer screen. I'm surprised Quinn hasn't stopped by yet today to cuddle with his wife, but maybe he's stuck in court doing lawyerly things.

"Hailey, I just talked to Mom and she wants me to remind you of the family lunch on Sunday."

She jumps at my voice and turns to smile at me. "I know, bring snickerdoodles."

We both laugh.

"Ashleigh and I talked about the family gathering this morning."

The Connor women sure are consistent in their commitment to family get-togethers.

"What did my sister say?"

Hailey giggles. "She's trying another new salad recipe."

I wrinkle my nose. "Oh boy! What's it made of this time? More kale?" The Connor men are not fans of my sister's healthy salads, but she keeps bringing them.

Hailey shakes her head. "This one's made from quinoa."

I frown. "What the heck is that?"

My office manager laughs. "It's a healthy grain that doesn't contain any gluten. Very popular right now. You need to keep an open mind, Max. I've heard it's quite tasty."

On that note, I turn to walk back into my office. "I'll look forward to trying it," I say over my shoulder.

I hear Hailey's laughter all the way back to my desk.

Chapter Four

Maddie

Worrying about my sort-of date with Max has made me anxious and unable to sleep. I tossed and turned all night, overanalyzing a simple lunch! As a result, I woke up this morning with a throbbing in my skull and nothing resolved in my head. What I need is someone else's perspective, someone I trust. My sister-in-law Rebecca is the perfect choice.

After Jack died, I avoided my in-laws for many months. It was simply too painful to see Rebecca and Jim with their new baby who was born only a few weeks before Jack died. Also, Jim resembles Jack in looks and mannerisms. There were too many memories and too many reminders of Jack for my broken heart to endure.

But, one day I bumped into Becca at the cemetery. She had baby Logan with her, and they were putting daisies on Jack's grave. I'd wondered on my previous visits who was putting the flowers out. The kind gesture brought tears to my eyes.

"Maddie, I hope you don't mind I'm putting flowers out for Jack," she said, nodding towards the bouquet in my own hands. "I miss him so much. And I miss you, too."

It was like a weight being lifted off my chest. I'd been hiding away from the exact people who could help me heal my heart. I hugged Becca for several minutes with tears streaming down my face. "Thank you for remembering Jack. I love the flowers you put out."

Five minutes of hugs and tears and our relationship picked right back up where it left off, like we had never disconnected. Becca is once again one of my best friends.

This morning I text Becca with an offer I know she can't refuse.

Maddie: I just made banana bread. How about I bring a loaf over and you make the coffee?

Becca: You know my weakness for your baked goods! Deal. Logan is just going down for a nap. Come over right away

Maddie: On my way with bread in hand!

Once I arrive at my in-laws, I see that they've started on the expansion to their house. Rebecca is almost eight months pregnant and they're running out of room in their cramped two-bedroom home. I knock rather than ring the bell since I don't want to wake Logan up.

My charming sister-in-law flings open the door, pulling me into a tight bear hug. Her belly is much bigger than the last time I saw her, and she has that mom-to-be glow. "Sweetie! Come on in and bring that delicious-smelling bread with you!"

I laugh as she puts her nose to the plastic-wrapped loaf in my hand.

We head back to the kitchen where Rebecca already has coffee brewing and mugs sitting on the round oak dining table. I sit down while she pours the coffee and hands me a knife, which I use to slice off two large hunks of the bread.

Sharing coffee with Becca is one of my favorite things. We're comfortable in each other's presence such that we can sip and enjoy the bread without a lot of small talk.

After several minutes, Becca says, "This bread is delicious Maddie, but when will the zucchini be ready? I just love your zucchini bread—the recipe with the chocolate chips." The ecstatic look on her face tells me she's really craving that once-a-year treat.

Chuckling, I reply, "My zucchini will be ready in August. Once it comes in, I'll have it running out of my ears. Zucchini bread, zucchini casseroles, fried zucchini . . . I'll share some with you." I look across the table at Becca, and we both break into laughter at the prolific vegetable that I can hardly give away.

After the laughing fit subsides, she wrinkles her nose. "I never know how to fix it. How about just giving me a loaf of zucchini bread and calling it good?"

I nod, knowing my sister-in-law isn't a skilled baker. Glancing around the room, I see a new painting gracing the wall next to the pantry. I point to it. "I see you have another one of Mother Henderson's works of art. When did she give you that one?"

Jack and Jim's mom is a self-taught painter. When the elder Hendersons retired and moved to Florida, Pearl had a lot of time on her hands and began creating masterpiece after masterpiece. Let's just say that she has the prolificness of Monet and the skill of a three-year-old.

Becca's lips draw together in a grimace. She obviously likes Pearl's artwork as much as I do. "That was a Christmas gift. Jim just hung it up last week. Don't you have any of her pieces?"

A slight blush crosses my face because I hate to admit where those paintings are right now. "Yeah, I have two."

My sister-in-law laughs. "Well, where are they? I didn't notice them last time I was at your house."

"In the hall closet behind the snow boots and Jack's bowling ball," I admit with chagrin.

A huge belly laugh emerges from Becca's small frame. "Lucky you she doesn't come visit anymore. We have to display her art or risk hurting her feelings."

I nod. "What do you think this latest piece is of? Are those sunflowers?" The giant yellow blobs seem like they might be blooms perched on greenish stems—albeit very misshapen.

We both tilt our heads, staring at the picture from different vantage points and trying to decide what it is. After a few minutes, I add, "Maybe you hung it the wrong direction. I think it needs to be horizontal."

Becca ponders that for a few seconds. "You might be right! I'll have Jim fix it when he gets home."

We look at each other and burst into more laughter, bending over and laughing so hard my stomach starts to hurt.

After we pull ourselves together, Becca asks, "Okay, Maddie, what do you need advice about?"

Am I that transparent? My shrewd coffee companion hits the nail on the head.

I fiddle with the handle of my coffee mug, trying to figure out how to broach the subject of dating another man to my dead husband's brother's wife. Awkward! Rather than beating around the bush, I blurt out, "I have a lunch date tomorrow and it has me tied up in knots."

A slow grin crosses Becca's face. She reaches across the table and squeezes my hand. "It's about time, Maddie. Jack would want you to move on," she says in the kindest, most understanding voice.

I sniffle as tears flood my eyes and I blink furiously. "You think so? I feel like I'm cheating on him."

She squeezes my hand again. "Don't ever think that. Who's your date?"

Blushing even more, I mumble, "One of my former students."

"Ha! Really? A younger man?" The excitement on her face is palpable.

I nod. "Yeah. He's about five years younger than me. You might know him . . . Max Connor?"

Her expression is priceless. "Hunky Max Connor?! Wow Maddie! Way to go, girl!" She looks like she wants to give me a high-five.

"So, you know him?"

Becca gets up and pours more coffee in both our mugs. "He's been here a couple of times, actually. Connor Construction is doing the addition on our house. They just poured the concrete yesterday." She points to the backyard where I see the newly poured footings. Grinning, Rebecca continues, "He's one fine-looking male specimen. All those muscles, that scruffy beard, the killer smile . . ." She trails off as if she's in her own world.

I clear my throat.

Becca blushes. "I'm just picturing him in my mind! Like you would Chris Hemsworth or Channing Tatum."

I laugh. "Right."

"Well, lucky you! Aren't you excited at the prospect of all that male magnetism focused on you?"

I squirm in my seat. "Actually, that's exactly what I'm worried about. How can that gorgeous man be interested in the nerdy math girl?"

Becca's mouth falls open. "Have you looked in the mirror? You're beautiful! Plus, you're smart as a tack. I bet he's counting his lucky stars you said you'll go out with him."

I bite my lip. "We definitely have chemistry. He said he's had a crush on me since he was my student five years ago."

She shrugs. "Most of your male students have crushes on you!"

True, and a little embarrassing. I think some of them take my calculus class just to get "the sexy professor" as they call me. That's the rumor I've heard anyway.

"Listen Maddie, you need to move on. I know it's difficult, but what are you waiting for? Jack's been dead over two years."

"I know," I say in a small voice. Despite the fact that time is marching on, my feelings and memories of Jack haven't faded. How do I move past all our good times? Guilt that I'm cheating on my husband overwhelms me every time I think about dating again. The trauma of his death surrounds me like a dark cloak I'm unable and maybe even unwilling to shed.

Rebecca picks up her mug and motions for me to do the same. She clinks her drink to mine in a toast. "To new beginnings."

Forcing a smile, knowing she's right, I participate in the toast. *Am I brave enough to let Jack go?*

Chapter Five

Max

Although I've been at the office for several hours, my lack of any progress on my to-do list annoys me. A certain professor has taken over all my brain space and won't let go.

The younger, brasher Max would be strutting around, patting himself on the back for scoring a date with Maddie. The current Max is anxious he'll mess something up on what may be my one opportunity to coax a way into her heart. Maddie's reluctance is a blow to my confidence. She didn't quite jump at the chance to go out with me despite my "friendship for now" speech. Have I been imagining that the attraction is mutual? Was my crush always one-sided?

I glance at the clock. *Finally.* Time to get going and take "the sexy professor" out to lunch. Grabbing my keys from the desk, I walk to the door. "Hailey, I'm off to lunch. I don't know when I'll be back. Just put any phone messages on my desk and I'll handle them when I return."

She squints up at me from whatever is so engrossing on her computer screen. Raising an eyebrow, she says, "Hot date? You look more dressed up than normal."

I give her a glare to discourage her delving any deeper into my attire and the lunch appointment. My silence probably says everything.

As I pull open the front door, the bells jingle and her words follow me out. "I know a good attorney who'll get the details out of you!"

~*~

Students slowly emerge from the classroom, mingling in small groups, their heads almost touching as they discuss the homework assignment. I remember those days! They ignore me hovering outside the door as they disappear down the hall.

Hailey is right—I took extra effort with what I'm wearing today. My newer blue jeans and ice blue button-down collar shirt beat my usual khaki shorts and T-shirt with my construction company logo plastered across the front. I upped my game hoping to entice my lunch companion to agree to a second date.

When I peek inside the classroom, there's one lone student asking Maddie questions as she packs up her massive bag with materials from the class. She politely answers his questions, but I see a small frown cross her face when he asks for more time to turn in the homework assignment. Maddie glances up and catches my eye, a blush spreading up her neck and across her cheeks. Interesting—the effect I have on her.

The student hurries off, almost plowing into me in his rush. He's still miffed after being told that the homework assignment is due in one week, without exception.

I stroll further into the room. "So, no exceptions for the homework assignment. Professor Maddie, you can be such a slave driver."

She puts her hands on her hips. "I have to be! Otherwise overly charming students try to get more time. As I remember," she reaches a hand up to her chin, "Max Connor tried to get an extension on his assignment because he had to milk cows for his grandfather. Or was it that he had to help his uncle frame a house? Oh, and he had to help his sister with her homework, giving him no time to complete his own." She shakes her head. "Such flimsy excuses."

Grinning, I walk right up to her, putting myself in her personal space. "Was I that bad?"

She doesn't back off, just laughs while putting the strap of her bag over her shoulder. "Yes!"

I wish I could take her in my arms and kiss that smirk off her face. Instead, I reach for the heavy bag. "Let me carry that. It looks like it weighs a ton."

Maddie shrugs, relinquishing the bag to me. As I put it on my shoulder, I realize how true my words are, the bag's surprising weight almost toppling me over. "What do you have in here? Bricks?"

"I'm old school and still carry textbooks with me. I have Calculus and Differential Equations textbooks in there."

I groan. "You're teaching Diffy Q this session as well?"

She laughs. "Yes, Mr. Connor. Would you like to join my class?"

Shaking my head, I reply, "No thank you."

"We can drop the bag in my office first, since it's so heavy."

I nod, taking her hand and pulling her along. "Right. I wouldn't want to get a back strain."

We both laugh as we head out the door.

~*~

Crossroads Deli is a little hole-in-the-wall place just outside campus. It gets its name because it's at the intersection of Highway 12 and County Road B. What used to be a cornfield has morphed into a small strip mall occupied with other campus-friendly merchants.

A teenager wearing far too much makeup greets us, thrusting two menus at us and scurrying off to sit other patrons. I drink in Maddie's presence while she reviews the menu. Today she's wearing a modest blue sundress. It shows off her tan arms while not revealing too much skin. Even though the dress goes to the top of her knees, I'm drooling at the long, tan legs shown off by the strappy sandals. Although, to be fair, she could wear a sack and I'd be enthralled.

27

Meeting my eyes across the tiny café table, she nods towards the menu lying in front of me. She raises an eyebrow because she's caught me staring at her.

"I'm enjoying the view."

Her cheeks turn an adorable pink and she points at the menu. "Do you know what you want?"

I nod. "Yes, you."

My reply surprises her and a darker blush spreads across her cheekbones. Maddie shakes her head like my mom does whenever one of her boys acts up. "I meant, what you want *to eat*." Again, she points towards my discarded menu.

I pick up the thick list of lunch choices even though I already know what food I want. The waitress plops down two glasses of ice water, sloshing it all over the table. Maddie grabs some napkins and neatly wipes up the spill.

"Whatcha want?" our teeny bopper server says while tapping her pen on the pad grasped in her hand. Her eyes are glued to me as if my date doesn't exist.

"Avocado turkey on wheat. Fresh fruit rather than chips." Maddie gives the waitress her menu back while the teeny bopper pops her gum and continues to stare at me.

"Corned beef on rye with chips," I reply, and the waitress gives me a coy smile, then scribbles on her pad. She rushes away into the kitchen.

"Do women of all ages flirt with you?" Maddie says with a giggle.

"She was flirting? How could you tell?"

An "are you kidding me" expression crosses the professor's face. "Well, let's see. She ignored me. She smiled at you and blushed when you said your order in that rumbly voice of yours."

I laugh. "Does my rumbly voice work on you? If so, I need to talk more."

She shakes her head and takes a sip of the ice water. "Tell me about work. How many homes are you putting up before the snow flies?"

My second favorite subject, after a certain math professor! I cross my arms and settle back in my chair. "We've got two new homes under construction, and I'm doing three house remodel projects. I've got a small crew, but we're booked until Thanksgiving with these projects. We'll focus mainly on remodelings over the winter though. I've got those booked out through next spring."

Maddie listens intently as I describe the home projects in more detail. One house is a million-dollar beauty being built overlooking the St. Croix river for a professional athlete with lots of money to spend.

"Wow. Building a place for a celebrity! How's that? Is he difficult to work with? Or is his wife overseeing the project?"

I chuckle. She's itching to know who it is.

"I signed an NDA, so I can't tell you who the client is. He isn't married, and he has a firm vision of what he wants. So far, he isn't a prima donna and we share the opinion that comfort and practicality win over flashiness. The home is going to be gorgeous—an *Architectural Digest* dream home, yet something a family can enjoy. We're using as many locally sourced materials as possible. The exterior stone came from near Redwing."

"I'm impressed! You're so passionate about what you do. That's great, Max."

I lean closer to her. "I even use some of those calculus principles you taught us every now and then!"

She fans her face like a Victorian maiden ready to faint. "I love it when a man talks about applying math!" Her eyes widen as she realizes what she just said. A blush spreads up her neck and cheeks.

Unfortunately, the waitress breaks the moment by setting an overflowing plate in front of each of us. She places a stack of napkins in the center of the table and disappears.

Maddie looks skeptically at her plate.

"Is something wrong with your order?"

"Aside from the fact that I got chips rather than fruit?" my companion says with a chuckle. "I guess our server was a little distracted by the Max factor."

I shrug because apparently I've become immune to females falling all over me. "Do you want to send it back?"

She grins. "Heavens no! I'll just figure out how I take a bite out of this huge sandwich and ignore the chips."

I pick up my corned beef and proceed to show her, taking a big bite and then chewing for several minutes. The deli special sauce runs down my hand. Maddie calmly hands me a napkin.

We eat in silence, focusing on the delicious, although messy, sandwiches. The professor figures out how to manipulate her sandwich by taking it apart and eating each side separately. Much less messy than my caveman approach. When she licks the special sauce from her fingers, my mouth goes dry. I tug the suddenly confining neck of my shirt collar. *Did they turn up the heat in here?*

After my plate is clean, Maddie asks for a box for the bottom portion of her sandwich while I give my credit card to the waitress. "So, what are your plans for the weekend?"

Maddie raises her eyes to mine. I've caught her off-guard again. "I'm very boring, Max. Weeding my garden and mowing the yard are the exciting activities planned for Saturday."

I smile. "Want help? You can weed and I can mow."

Uncertainty crosses her face. She bites her bottom lip for a few seconds. "Okay, but you really don't need to help. I can mow my own yard."

I reach across the table and squeeze her hand. "What's the fun in that?"

She giggles like a schoolgirl. This courtship is going to be enjoyable.

"What time should I come over? Oh, and I'll need your address."

Maddie rolls her eyes, then texts me her address. "How about ten? It won't be too warm by then."

I want to say *it's a date* but I don't want to scare her off. "I'll be there."

Smiling, Maddie squeezes my hand back. "I'll have coffee ready."

Chapter Six

Maddie

I've never worried over what to wear to weed the garden like I'm doing today. My faded capris and ratty T-shirt with "I'm a Math Teacher Of Course I Have Problems" splashed across the front don't seem appropriate when a sexy man is helping me with yardwork. Just the thought makes my heart pound and my palms sweat. This is ridiculous!

I finally decide on blue jean shorts and a scoop-neck blue T-shirt. They showcase my physical assets without showing them off too much. I pull my hair into a ponytail to keep it off my face. The style has the added benefit of making me look younger. Sighing, I glance at myself in the mirror as I realize that this is the first time since Jack's death I've taken special care with what I'm wearing. As Becca reminded me yet again this morning, "You have to move on. Jack would want you to."

Ding! Dong!

The sound makes my heart rate skyrocket. My sweet border collie perks up his ears and trots over to the door, sitting patiently for me to answer. The time of reckoning has come. I take a deep breath and open the door. Unfortunately, the breath I just took swooshes out when I see Max. The ability to speak more than one syllable words deserts me and I sputter, "Uh, come in."

He looks like he stepped off the cover of a romance novel. His five o'clock shadow emphasizes his strong jaw, giving him a rugged yet sexy look. Khaki shorts enhance his strong thighs and showcase a manly pair of legs that my hands want to roam over. But it's the black T-shirt that does me in. It clings to every muscle in his broad chest. The sleeves bulge, displaying a set of drool-worthy biceps. *Did I just lick my lips?*

"Who's this?" Max says, addressing the black and white, tail-wagging bundle of fur dancing around our feet. Max bends over and pets him on the head.

The sight of the big man gently petting my beloved dog makes my eyes tear up. I clear my suddenly dry throat. "His name is Fibonacci. I call him Fibi for short."

Max straightens back up to his full height and looks at me. "As in the sequence?" A smile splits across his face.

I shrug and giggle. "What do you expect from a math professor?"

Max laughs. "He's beautiful. A border collie, right?"

I kneel and Fibi puts his soft head into my chest. "Yep, he's full blooded. Bred for Agility competitions. Three years ago, he was the top Agility dog in the state." I beam like a proud parent.

Max joins me in the kneeling position. "No kidding? Did you train him? Do you and Fibi still compete?"

Our hands touch as we both pet the gorgeous animal. I pull back, my hand and arm tingling from the brief contact. My brain struggles to get back in gear and answer the questions. "He was professionally trained. We got him when he was a one-year-old." My voice cracks a little at the memory of Jack bringing home the cute dog as an anniversary gift. When my sweet husband put the bundle of fur in my arms, it was love at first sight. I remember Jack's laughter as he watched Fibi and I training and how amateurish we were at first. Once we mastered the sport, Jack was our biggest fan whether we won a ribbon or not. A surge of sadness overwhelms my heart, reminding me that I'm still not over my husband. "I don't compete anymore. It was too much, traveling on weekends after Jack died."

Max reaches over and squeezes my arm. We share the emotional moment in silence. I swipe a tear from the corner of my eye and quickly stand. "Would you like some coffee while we plan our yardwork strategy?"

After I pour two mugs, we settle into the comfortable rattan chairs on the back patio—one of my favorite spots. The awning provides shade as we look out over my expansive lawn. *Maybe I should have mentioned my one-acre lot when Max volunteered to mow?*

"This is a big yard! I love the mature oak trees. How do you keep up with all the maintenance?" Max raises his eyebrow.

"I love working in the yard. You'll be happy to learn there's a John Deere riding lawn mower in that shed over there." I point towards the little red utility shed at the back of the property.

Max laughs. "Good to know."

Once we've finished our coffee, I take him to the garden plot at the far end of the lot. Fibi races ahead while we walk at a slower pace.

"These are my pride and joy." I point to the raised beds. Zucchini, tomatoes, and pole beans fill the first bed, where the zucchini is fighting to take over. One of my tasks today will be to contain the zucchini to its side of the patch. The second bed contains strawberries, carrots, onions, green peppers, and leaf lettuce that's already run its course—the hot weather wilting it on the vine.

Max surveys the garden while Fibi sniffs at the tomato plants. "Fibi, get out of there!" I say and shoo him away. The tomatoes are still green; I don't expect any to be ripe until late August. A few red berries hide under the strawberry plant leaves. I'll pick them today so they don't rot.

"Maddie, this is impressive! My parents always plant a big garden, but they have lots of help between me and my brothers and sister. How do you do all this by yourself?"

His words pierce my heart, even though he didn't intend to. "When Jack died, I vowed that nothing would change. We always put out a garden and I was adamant to keep doing so. The first year I struggled using the tiller in the spring and running the weed whacker, since Jack always did that." I frown at the memory of me grappling with the heavy tiller and accidentally cutting a bush down to the roots with the weed whacker. "Eventually I learned how to do everything on my own." My voice trails off and I can't hide the sadness that being a widow makes me feel. I never imagined myself without Jack until fate stepped in.

He shakes his head, rubbing my arm. "I keep bringing up sad memories for you. I'm sorry."

I grasp his hand, stilling its motion. "I'm sorry too. There's so much of Jack in this place, it's difficult not to bump into his memory all the time. I've thought about moving, but . . ." My voices trails off and I bite my trembling lower lip.

Max pulls me into a tight hug. His warm body encases me, providing comfort while at the same time my body shivers at the delicious male contact.

"It's okay. I understand," he says quietly. We stand hugging for several minutes while he rubs my back.

After what could be five seconds or five minutes, I'm not sure, Max whispers in my ear, "We have an audience." Fibi sits at my feet, tilting his head and watching us.

I nod and giggle, pulling slowly out of Max's embrace. Our eyes meet and I desperately want to kiss him. Instead I say, "Shall we get to work? I'll get the lawn mower out of the shed."

Max grins. "Men love riding lawn mowers! Show me the way."

~*~

Watching Max mowing makes my heart do flip flops. He's a sweaty mess by the time he's done—all male and sexy. I hand him a bottle of water and he chugs it. My eyes can't stop watching those glorious chest muscles and the sweaty T-shirt clinging to them. His biceps flex as he tilts the bottle to his mouth. *I have it bad for this guy. Am I just crushing on him or is there something more?*

Pulling my eyes back up to his face, I see he's watching me watch him. A blush spreads up my neck. "Would you like to clean up a little? I can give you one of Jack's T-shirts to wear?"

The mention of Jack's name puts a damper on the moment. I see a small frown cross Max's face, but he hides it quickly. *Why do I keep bringing up my dead husband?*

Max goes to the powder room down the hall. I lay a T-shirt outside the closed door and tell him it's there. Then I hustle into the kitchen in case he opens the door and I get to see his bare chest. Gulp.

I'm standing at the island cutting up fresh strawberries when Max reappears. Our eyes lock for a few seconds. His hair is damp, and he's wearing the green T-shirt that's almost too small for him. Max must be bulkier than Jack was.

"Hopefully the Polish shower did the trick and I don't smell too bad," Max says with a sexy grin. He's holding his sweaty T-shirt, so I give him a plastic grocery bag, then he bags the shirt and sets it beside the front door. "You have a nice place here, Maddie. I like the layout and kitchen updates," Max says when he returns.

I smile. "We had the kitchen remodeled four years ago. Funny thing, your uncle did the job."

His eyes widen. "So, this is Connor Construction work? No wonder it looks so great!" We both laugh.

Pointing around the room, I continue, "I love the granite countertops, stainless appliances, and dark cherry cabinets. Very warm and cozy. The huge island is a big improvement from what we had before. They moved the back wall out about ten feet and that really opened up the space."

Max nods and then helps me carry our food to the back patio. Even though the temps are in the 90s, the ceiling fan keeps the space cool.

I quickly realize that Max can really chow down the food. His ham and swiss sandwich is consumed before I've taken three bites. I'm not used to feeding a man anymore and I forgot how much they can eat.

"Do you want another sandwich?" I nod towards his empty plate.

He chuckles. "No, I'm good. Just enjoying this iced tea. It hits the spot on a hot day like today."

I pass him the bag of potato chips, which he snacks on while I continue downing my sandwich. A comfortable silence settles between us as he sips his tea and I finish the ham and swiss.

"You did a great job with the mowing, being it was your first time . . ." I cringe inwardly at the implication that I expect Max to mow for me again in the future. Pulling my foot out of my mouth, I continue. "Not that I'm saying there will be another time or anything . . . The yard is oddly shaped and a little tricky to mow . . ." I keep fumbling around with my words as embarrassment floods my cheeks. I close my eyes and blow out a quick breath. *Stop talking!*

"Maddie, it's okay. I know what you meant." Max reaches across the table and squeezes my hand.

Our eyes meet. His smile is so sweet I want to burst into tears at my awkwardness. I'm out of practice at having a man around. Maybe this is just second date jitters. Or maybe it's something more.

I hop up to retrieve the strawberries and ice cream from the kitchen. Max follows me with our empty plates and I plow into him in my rush to the fridge to get the dessert. He grasps my shoulders, then gently takes both my hands in his.

I tilt my head back to look at him.

"Hey, Maddie. Just chill. I'm having a wonderful time being with you. Why are you so nervous around me?" He strokes my fingers; the tingles run all the way up my arms. I try to pull away, but he holds on, waiting for my answer.

I look down at my feet for a few beats, then back up. "Max, I'm so sorry. I've repeatedly mentioned my dead husband, even giving you his shirt to wear." I nod towards the green T-shirt staring me in the face. My eyes fill with tears as I stare into his amazing blue ones. "You must think I'm crazy."

He shakes his head. "No, not crazy. Your husband's memory is everywhere around us, I get that. All I want is for you to give me a chance . . . Give us a chance," he says with such a sincere and heartbreaking look in his eyes.

I swallow as a tear trickles down my cheek. This gorgeous man is standing right here, yet I can't get Jack out of my head. This was a bad idea.

Max wipes my tears off with his thumb. "It's time for me to go. I want to keep seeing you, but next time let's go out someplace that doesn't remind you so much of Jack. How about we go out for dinner next week?" The smile he gives me makes my knees weak.

My mind whirls with how to answer the question. I want to go out with him, but I'm scared to do so. I feel like a gawky freshman who finally caught the senior's eye. My palms are sweaty, I'm a nervous wreck, and my words desert me most of the time. On top of that, I bring up another guy over and over. This first venture into dating post-Jack feels like a disaster.

What am I more afraid of—moving on or falling for Max?

My gut tells me it's the latter. Fear takes over, though, and I blurt out a handy excuse, "Today has taught me that I'm not ready to date *anyone* yet, Max. I'm so sorry."

He looks me intently in the eyes as if he's searching my soul. Disappointment crosses his face for a fleeting second then it's gone. "I'm not giving up, Maddie. I'm a patient man and you're worth waiting for."

With those words, he strides out of the kitchen and I hear the click of the front door as it closes behind him. Max is stirring up feelings that I thought were buried. He makes me want something that I haven't wanted since Jack died. *Did I just ruin it by being afraid?*

Chapter Seven

Max

Saturday flew by—my time with Maddie was much too short. I crave her like chocolate, and the craving won't go away no matter how many times I'm with her. Watching her weed the garden in those sexy shorts and tight T-shirt made me almost run over one of the lilac bushes at the edge of the lawn. Thankfully I didn't embarrass myself by doing that.

I hear the office bells jingle. Hailey giggles and then I hear distant noises for several minutes. I stay in my office to avoid breaking up the kissing session that my sister-in-law and brother are undoubtedly having in the front office. I try to tune out the sighs and other sounds coming from that part of the building. As long as customers don't come in, I'm fine with them doing a little canoodling, assuming they keep it PG-13.

After several minutes, Quinn appears in my doorway. His hair is mussed, and his T-shirt is not neatly tucked into his shorts like it usually is. I chuckle at the sight.

"You have lipstick on your face." I point towards my cheek.

My brother settles into one of the guest chairs across from my desk, rubbing his cheek with his thumb.

"Other side."

He grins, making a big show of cleaning both his cheeks with his thumbs. He raises an eyebrow. "Did I get it?"

I shake my head, giving him a smirk. Hailey and Quinn act like two teenagers even though they've been married for ten months.

"What's the reason for your visit, other than to neck with your wife?"

Quinn laughs, a booming laugh coming from deep inside his broad chest. "Kissing Hailey is just a bonus! I came to ask my brother about his hot date on Saturday."

I frown. Word travels fast in the Connor family. I casually mentioned to Ashleigh that I was busy helping a friend with yardwork on Saturday. How did the entire family find out and why do they assume it was a date?

"It wasn't a date," I clarify. "Just helping a friend with yardwork."

It's Quinn's turn to smirk. "Is the friend named Madeleine Henderson?"

My mouth drops open. "How did you find out?"

Another laugh bursts from my brother. "Mom might have mentioned to Hailey that you had a lunch date with the professor. Then when Ash spilled the beans about your helping a friend on Saturday, we put two and two together."

If Maddie thinks our sort-of relationship is on the down low, she's in for a big surprise. This is what it's like living in a small town. Gossip spreads like wildfire and everyone knows everyone's business.

I sigh. "What exactly did Mom say?"

"She's already penciling the wedding in her daily planner!"

We both laugh, knowing that statement isn't too far off the truth. Mom can be a little overzealous in her desire for all her children to marry and have kids.

Speaking of which . . . "How's the baby project coming?"

Quinn leans forward in his chair, as if to tell me a secret. Instead he says in a boisterous voice, "Good try deflecting, Brother. But it won't work. Spill on your date with Professor Maddie!"

Rolling my eyes, I reply, "I helped mow her yard. End of story."

Quinn shakes his head. "Come on, we're family. I promise not to tell anyone else other than Hailey."

I shrug, deciding to tell my brother everything. Maybe he can add new perspective to my predicament. "We get along great. She's fun to be with, even if I sweated like a pig mowing her yard.

Sadly, though, she's not over her husband's death yet. It was like he was there with us. There were so many memories of him, I felt like a third wheel."

A sad expression crosses Quinn's face. "That must be tough for both of you. I'm sure you'll help her move on, though. You're not trying to erase the memory of him, just adding new memories of you."

I ponder Quinn's wise words. When I left Maddie's on Saturday, I was discouraged and depressed. I've waited for her for five years, yet I'm not certain whether she can get over her dead husband. I need to help Maddie see that moving on doesn't mean she's cutting Jack out of her heart, rather she's letting me share a spot with him. Maddie has one of the biggest hearts I know, surely she can make room for me.

"If we weren't at her house, it would have been easier to not have Jack's name pop up every other sentence," I say with a sigh. "Unfortunately, right before I left, she pumped the brakes pretty hard on going out with me again any time soon. I feel the chemistry between us and know she does, too. I think that's what's scaring her."

My brother smiles. "Don't give up! She might need time, but you need to keep reminding her of your interest. There's other ways to get her attention than dating." He wiggles his eyebrows then yells, "Hailey!"

Hailey pops her head in the door. Quinn pats his lap and she sits down while he plants another kiss on her cheek. "Give my brother some advice on how to court Professor Maddie. She's a little scared and gun-shy right now. What do you suggest?"

The blonde giggles. "My husband flirts with me all day long by texting me sweet, funny stuff. Do you have her number? Text her and let her know you're thinking of her."

Quinn nods enthusiastically at the suggestion. I grin.

Hailey pauses, then continues. "Send her flowers. Remember when Quinn's ex came to town? He brought me the biggest bouquet of flowers I'd ever seen, and we made up." She smiles, giving Quinn a quick kiss on the lips.

I hold up my hand. "Okay, I've got some ideas." I need to break up the lovefest and get back to work.

Quinn whispers in Hailey's ear and she blushes to her hairline. When he says something further, she nods.

I raise an eyebrow, wondering what they're talking about. After my brother starts fidgeting with his shirt collar, I know he's either nervous or excited.

"Well? What's the big secret?" I prod, because the suspense is now making me nervous.

"We're pregnant!" Quinn declares loudly while high-fiving his wife.

I stand and give them both a hug. "Congratulations! When did you find out?"

"Yesterday," Hailey says with a laugh.

"Don't tell Mom or Ash. We want to make a big announcement at the next family dinner," Quinn adds.

"I understand. It's your news to tell, but I'm honored you told me. Uncle Max has a nice ring to it, don't you think?" The news makes me imagine Maddie and me with two kids, two dogs (Fibi plus one), and a yard with a picket fence.

The elated couple laughs, walking out hand in hand. Even though I'm happy for them, it reminds me how far I still need to go to win a certain professor's heart.

Chapter Eight

Maddie

I'm a mess. After Max left on Saturday, I sat on the couch and sobbed for forty-five minutes. Part of me wants to jump in with both feet to a relationship with him. The other part is scared out of my mind.

Jack Henderson was my first boyfriend. He's the only man I ever dated. The only man I've ever been intimate with. While Jack was handsome and attractive in his own way, our relationship never had the heart-pounding, pulse-skyrocketing emotions I feel every time I'm with Max. Don't get me wrong, I loved my husband deeply. What I feel for Max pushes me into new, terrifying territory.

Like I said, I'm a mess.

Yoga class is just what I need to take my mind off that sexy but confusing man and calm my nerves. I arrive a few minutes early and take my spot near the back of the room. As I roll out my mat, a pretty blonde wearing blue leggings and a white tank top approaches me. I've seen her in class many times and we nod and smile at each other, but we've never spoken.

"Are you Madeleine Henderson?" she says while rolling her mat down beside mine.

"Yes, I am! And you are . . . ?" My brow wrinkles as I wonder if she's previously introduced herself and I've forgotten her name.

She laughs while we both take a seat on our mats. "We haven't met before. I'm Hailey Connor. I'm married to Max's brother, and I'm the office manager at Connor Construction."

Everything clicks into place. Professor Bolton mentioned Hailey that day Max first visited me. She started classes last fall.

"Nice to meet you! I've seen you in yoga class before, but I'm sorry I didn't introduce myself sooner." I feel sloppy in my old black leggings and oversized T-shirt. Why didn't I wear something nicer?

Hailey smiles. "No problem! I understand my brother-in-law helped you with yardwork on Saturday. Max is such a great guy!" Her brown eyes dart to the side then focus on mine as she leans in slightly. "Between you and me, he's smitten with you. He'd kill me if he knew I was telling you this!"

I try to keep a poker face. "Did he mention me to you? How did you know about Saturday?" My questions sound like something a teenager would ask, and I cringe.

She laughs and starts pulling her gear out of her bag. "My husband is a big blabber mouth. Max confided in him that he was at your place. I hear you have a big yard! I'm glad Max helped with the mowing."

I can tell she knows more than she's letting on, but I don't divulge any more details. "Yeah, he was a huge help."

Hailey leans in towards me again. "When Max found out I started classes at the community college, he mentioned you. That was last September and I could tell even then he had a crush on you. A big one." She winks.

I keep silent and don't probe for more details, yet Hailey plows ahead, praising several more of her boss's positive traits. "Charming, handsome, smart, and a great boss to work for" comes across loud and clear.

The instructor greets the class and kicks off the session, distracting Hailey from any more PR work for Max. After fifty minutes we're all sweaty and my muscles are protesting. I quickly roll up my mat and when I'm ready to leave, Hailey says, "I'll let Max know I saw you! Have a nice day."

Did Max put her up to singing his praises?

~*~

I hop in the shower as soon as I get home. The conversation with Hailey plays around in my mind. Her praise for Max was as subtle as a bulldozer. I squirm, wondering if I can resist the full court press that Max and his team are apparently putting towards getting us together.

Summer semester is a light load for me—I only teach three days a week. With today being one of my days off, I tackle some cleaning chores that I've let go for a few weeks. Dusting and cleaning the bathrooms are not my favorite activities.

Ding! Dong!

The loud bell rings just as I start dusting the shelves in my bedroom. I'm not expecting anyone, but chances are good that my sweet—but nosy—neighbor Gloria Robinson will stop over today. I'm sure she saw Max mowing my yard on Saturday. I've been expecting her to come ringing ever since.

Opening the door, a young twenty-something guy wearing a baggy T-shirt and shorts is standing on my porch holding the most gorgeous bouquet of sunflowers and daisies. He grins at me over the giant arrangement. "Madeleine Henderson?" he asks while adjusting the heavy vase in his hands.

"Yes," I reply with a goofy smile on my face.

"These are for you." He thrusts the vase into my hands. "Have a nice day!" He runs back to the delivery van parked in the driveway before I can even say thank you.

I hold the beautiful flowers carefully while I walk into the dining room, then place them on the oak dining table. The expensive cut-crystal vase sparkles in the sunlight, and the yellow sunflowers and white daisies give the room a cheery feel.

I pull out the card tucked into the arrangement and read it.
Thinking of you –Max

I clasp the card to my heart. How can I resist this guy? Jack rarely bought me flowers and when he did, he went with the traditional red roses, which aren't my favorite. Max, on the other hand, hit the nail on the head with the sunflowers and daisies.

Grabbing my cell phone, I send a text.

Maddie: Thank you for the beautiful flowers! You shouldn't have done that (smiley face Emoji)

Several minutes later, a reply lights up my screen.

Max: I drove by a field of sunflowers this morning on my way to one of our construction sites and I thought of you (heart Emoji)

Maddie: I love them! They look wonderful on my dining table.

Max: Think of me every time you walk by (winking Emoji)

I sigh as mixed feelings bombard me again. Do I want safe and comfortable Professor Bolton (who now repeatedly asks me out to dinner whenever we eat lunch) or terrifying and sexy Max? Mr. Connor is very persistent, and I may lose my heart to him yet.

~*~

After the flower surprise, I can't stop thinking about Max. Was I too hasty in trying to discourage him? Why am I not ready to date yet even though Jack's been dead for over two years? All these questions swirl around in my brain, making my head hurt.

Thank goodness for my hair appointment. I love getting my hair washed and trimmed; it will give me a chance to relax and not think about the sexy Connor brother.

My usual stylist Natalie is on vacation, so I'm booked with Valerie today. She greets me in the waiting area and takes me over to her station. Once I'm seated, she puts a giant lime green plastic cape around me and rotates the chair so I'm looking in the mirror at her.

"What are we doing today? Something new?" She smiles with encouragement.

I laugh. "No, just a trim."

Valerie nods, then shampoos my hair with some wonderful lavender-smelling shampoo. I relax at the washing station, enjoying the pampering.

Once she starts the trim, Valerie becomes chatty. I don't mind, but Natalie generally lets me relax and enjoy the cut, not engaging in much conversation. I mostly ignore Valerie's commentary and let myself daydream.

"One of my usual customers is Ashleigh Connor. She came in just before you."

My eyes snap open and my brows pull together. Oh no. Where is this conversation going? "Really? I don't know her personally. I'm friends with her brother."

Valerie laughs. "According to Ash, you're dating her brother Max. I must say, he's one hot tamale! Lucky you."

My face turns beet red. *Is today Max Connor promotion day?* "We're not really dating—"

Val cuts me off before I can explain further. "Sweetie, when a man does yardwork on a Saturday for you, he's serious!" Does everyone in town know about that? Valerie clearly can't tell how uncomfortable I'm getting as she plows on. "Max and I graduated in the same class in high school. He's such a great guy! Most women in Connor's Grove would donate a kidney if they thought that would get Max's attention."

I nod, then remember that Val has sharp scissors in her hands and she's cutting my hair. My head movement quickly stops. "I'll keep that in mind" is my lame response.

She stares at me in the mirror while continuing to snip hair. "Honey, if you don't go after him, someone else will. My advice is to grab that sweet man and never let him go!" Her laugh echoes throughout the shop. Heads turn towards us and my blush deepens.

Though it's a relief to be done with my trim and away from Valerie's exuberance, once I exit the salon, I can't help but grin. All this marketing going on for Max. First Hailey, then Valerie. Who's next?

On the way home, I stop by the grocery store for milk and OJ. Do I need to put on a disguise, so the checkout lady or bagger kid doesn't flag me down and expound on Max's wonderful qualities? I chuckle to myself as I rush through the store wearing sunglasses and a baseball cap pulled low over my forehead. I escape without hearing more accolades. None of the Connors must have stopped by the grocery store this morning.

Driving home after safely escaping the store without any more of Mr. Connor's fans cornering me, I ponder the differences between William and Max.

During lunch with Professor Bolton two days ago, I'd noticed traits that I hadn't recognized when I was thinking of him merely as a colleague. We were sitting in the student union eating our usual—a Greek salad for me and Rueben on rye for him. The fact that we both always order the same thing tells me that neither of us is very adventurous.

"Did you see the fall session class assignments yet?" William asks. The scowl on his face tells me he isn't happy about it.

Munching on my bite of salad, I shake my head. Once I swallow, I add, "Haven't read my email yet today."

The scowl deepens and he huffs, "Well, I was assigned Linear Algebra and Multivariable Calculus on top of my three Calc 2 classes. Guess I'm the workhorse in the department." He sighs loudly as if the weight of the world is on his shoulders.

I never noticed before that he's such a whiner. But reflecting back, his "poor me" attitude is a common theme. Putting a sympathetic look on my face, I reply, "I could offer to pick up one of your Calc 2 classes."

William shakes his head an emphatic "no." "Calc 2 is typically taught by the more experienced professors in the department."

I remember my mouth hanging open in shock at his belittling remark. At the time I tried to shrug it off as him just being grumpy over the schedule. But the more I think about it, the more I question whether he respects me or not.

Despite his foot-in-mouth comments, I usually enjoy lunches with less-than-perfect Professor Bolton. He's like a comfortable pair of house slippers with a hole in the toe, where Max is like a flashy pair of LeBron James basketball shoes. When I'm ready to date again, which one would I rather go with?

Chapter Nine

Max

Operation "win Maddie's heart" is going well. She loved the flowers I sent her, Hailey cornered her during yoga class to extol my many virtues, and Ash figured out Maddie was getting a haircut and got her stylist to sing my praises. Don't even ask how she pulled that off, but Ash can be rather nosy. I'm sure Mom has something planned; I just don't know about it yet.

The Connor family can be charmingly pushy. You don't even realize what's happening until it's too late. Although I didn't ask for their help, I'll take what I can get as long as it convinces Maddie to take a chance on us. The rest will be up to me.

While my daily texts are mostly silly, Maddie is getting into them. I texted her a traditional algebra word problem today, you know the type that says "Two trains start from the same point and travel in the same direction. The second leaves 48 minutes later than the first, travels 10 miles per hour faster, and overtakes the first train in 4 hours. Find the speed of each train."

She texted back, "Train 1 is going 50 mph and Train 2 is going 60 mph" in 23 seconds flat. Yes, I admit I was timing her. This woman is smart, or she solves a lot of train problems.

Being a smarty-pants, I texted back, "What about Train 3?"

She replied, "Train 3 is still sitting at the station waiting for you to get on board." Followed by a string of eye roll Emojis.

Game on! I make it my mission to find a math problem that will stump the lovely professor.

Sometimes my texts aren't silly stuff. Yesterday I took a photo of a doe and her fawn in a field near Stillwater. The sun was just coming up and there was a light fog hanging near the ground. It was an amazing photo, so I just had to share it with Maddie. She texted back a string of hearts—hopefully directed at me and not just the deer.

So far, I haven't pushed to schedule another date. Maddie said she wasn't ready, so I'm giving her time. As Quinn told me a few days ago, "Absence makes the heart grow fonder, so let her come to you. Give her love and attention from afar. She'll be at your door in no time." Since I've already waited five years for her, I guess a few more weeks or even a month won't hurt.

I keep telling myself that anyway.

Hailey pops her head in my doorway, pulling me from researching another algebra problem for the professor.

"Quinn said he's running fifteen minutes late at the courthouse, so he'll meet us at your parents' house. Can I get a ride with you?"

"Sure. We don't want to be late for Dad's BBQ spareribs!" Even though my parents don't know it, tonight's family dinner is the big announcement from Quinn and Hailey. "When do you plan to make the baby announcement?"

My office manager chews on her lower lip. "We'll wait until after dinner because I think your mom will be too excited to eat once she finds out."

"That's the understatement of the year, Hailey!"

She giggles nervously and shuts down her computer while I grab my keys and a set of blueprints I need for a meeting at a jobsite tomorrow morning. Hailey follows me to my pickup truck, where I help her inside.

"I haven't asked how you've been feeling? You look great, by the way."

She smiles and nods while I navigate Connor's Grove Friday night traffic. Nothing like the big city, but still requires my full attention.

"I'm nauseous first thing in the morning. Quinn brings me saltine crackers and 7 Up to help settle my stomach. That's been working, and I can usually keep the crackers down. I sip 7 Up during the day if I feel queasy."

I'd noticed the sudden addition of 7 Up to our office mini fridge. I grunt, keeping my eyes glued to the road.

"Is that too much information, Max?" She laughs. "By the look on your face, you really didn't want an honest answer to your question, did you?"

I turn beet red at my sister-in-law's teasing. "Actually, I figured you would say you were feeling fine and we'd move on."

She giggles. "I'm feeling fine."

We both laugh.

When I turn onto Highway 12, the traffic lightens. Turning my head towards Hailey, I say, "Seriously, Hailey, if you don't feel like coming into the office, just call and let me know. I want my sister-in-law to be happy and my nephew to be healthy."

She snorts. "You and Quinn are on this boy kick! What if we're having a girl?"

"We'll teach her to play football and cheer for the Vikings, of course."

Hailey shakes her head sharply. "Um. Not happening. I'm going to buy her a green and yellow onesie and a tiny piece of plastic cheese for her head. I plan on making her a true Packers fan."

"Grandma Connor isn't going to like that. She'll insist you dress her in purple and gold with a tiny Viking helmet."

We both laugh. The rivalry between Hailey and the rest of the Connor family is well known. Every time the Vikings play the Packers, Hailey dresses in full Packers gear while the rest of the family dresses in Vikings clothing. We have a great time teasing her about her choice of team. Unfortunately, in recent years, the

Packers have beat the Vikings almost every game, giving Hailey bragging rights for the season.

As I turn into my parent's long driveway, I glance over at Hailey. "Even if she's a Packer's fan, we'll all love her just the same."

Hailey smiles. "I know."

~*~

The entire Connor family has turned up for dinner, including our almost-never-in-attendance brother Jacob. Quinn must have threatened him if he didn't show.

Ashleigh meets us at the door. "Hailey and Max are here!" she shouts. "Where's Quinn?"

"He's right behind us, he got tied up in court but he's on his way," Hailey replies.

We follow our noses to the kitchen where Mom and Nana are both hurrying around preparing what looks to be a luscious dinner. The island is overflowing with potato salad, coleslaw, Ashleigh's infamous quinoa/kale/spinach salad, baked beans bubbling in a crock pot, two rhubarb pies, and a plate of brownies. Dad is manning the grill on the back deck, turning the spareribs and slathering them with his "special" sauce (aka Kraft Hickory Smoke BBQ). His face is red since it's 90 degrees out. Jacob's sipping on a beer and chatting with Dad. *Think I'll stay in the air-conditioning.*

"Smells great!" Hailey says, placing her hand against her stomach. Since she confided in me that she's nauseous sometimes I'm sure the aromas are driving her crazy, but she's too nice to not compliment my mother.

"Yeah, Mom, you've outdone yourself! This amount of food could feed an army." I can't resist the teasing comment.

Mom laughs. "Don't want anyone to go hungry!"

"I'm here!" Quinn yells from the living room. Seconds later he pops around the corner into the kitchen carrying another six-pack of beer, a two-liter bottle of root beer for Ash and a two-liter of 7 Up. He must be worried about Hailey getting an upset stomach because none of us like 7 Up. He walks over to his wife, pulling her into a noisy kiss.

"Get a room you two!" Ash says as she flicks a dishtowel towards Quinn and hits him in the butt.

Quinn gets Ash in a head lock, giving her a knuckle rub on the head. Those two are always fake fighting with each other. I say it stems from the fact that Quinn is oldest and was always very protective of his baby sister. Ash resented him trying to protect her from overly zealous boyfriends. He was more of a deterrent to Ash dating than Dad ever was.

Minutes later Dad and Jacob come inside, carrying two platters stacked with the BBQ spareribs. They sit them on the dining room table. Everyone carries a dish in from the kitchen, jockeying for positions in the center of the table, then we scramble for our seats.

When Hailey first came to Thanksgiving dinner with Quinn, she looked a little overwhelmed at the boisterous Connor family. Now she's one of us, reaching for a sparerib before Mom's even said the blessing.

"Quiet everyone! Join hands."

Quinn, Jacob, and I snicker because Mom always says the same thing every time. Unless it's a holiday, she usually gives her version of the Johnny Appleseed blessing, as we call it, which she does today. "The Lord's been good to us, so we thank him for giving us the things we need, the sun, the rain, and the apple seed. Amen."

Sometimes she even sings it, which thankfully she didn't do today.

Amens echo around the table, then we pass dishes, loading up our plates. Ash teases Jacob for not taking any of her healthy salad. He grudgingly takes the bowl back, adding one spoonful to his plate just to appease her.

Hailey and Quinn have their heads together and are giggling about something. He's probably teasing her about the amount of potato salad on her plate. Who can blame her since she's eating for two?

After several minutes of silverware clanking against china plates while we enjoy the delicious food, Ash says in a loud voice so everyone can hear, "Max, how's it going wooing the professor?"

Silence descends around the table and all eyes turn to me. Nana winks. Mom beams. And Gramps keeps eating spareribs.

I shrug. How much do I tell them? "She liked the flowers I sent her."

Mom oohs. Dad grunts and says, "Most women like flowers, Max."

Several people chuckle at that comment, including me.

"Apparently all the Connor women have taken to trying to help me with my love life." I send a pointed glare first at Hailey and then Ashleigh. Both snicker and look pleased with themselves.

Once the plates are empty, Ash and Hailey clear the table and bring in the desserts. When they've returned to their chairs, Quinn clears his throat and stands.

"Hailey and I have an announcement." All eyes now turn to him. He squeezes Hailey's hand and she smiles up at him with such adoration it makes my heart hurt. *Will Maddie ever look at me that way?*

"We're expecting a baby. He or she is due next March."

Chaos ensues as if Quinn dropped a bomb in the middle of the table. Mom squeals and runs over to hug Hailey and Quinn, shouting that they're having a little Leprechaun. Nana wipes a tear from her eye. Ash dances around the table singing, "I'm going to be an aunt."

Jacob and I stand so we can slap Quinn on the back a couple of times. "Congrats, Big Brother!" we say in unison. Dad and Gramps ignore the celebration and continue eating their rhubarb pie.

Once everything settles back down and everyone has returned to their seats, Dad says, "I wondered what the 7 Up was for."

Chapter Ten

Maddie

My head's stuck in the closet, digging out all our old agility equipment. Fibi sniffs at every piece I find. His tail wags, telling me he also missed the competitions. After Jack died, I didn't have the drive or desire to compete anymore. The discussion with Max inspired me to try to compete again. Max is good for me in several ways; I just haven't let myself acknowledge it yet.

Ding! Dong!

I jump, bumping my forehead on the closet rod filled with winter apparel. Rubbing my head, I rush to answer the door. I'm not expecting anyone this Saturday morning.

Peering through the side window I see my nosy neighbor Gloria standing on the doorstep. Here comes the Spanish Inquisition . . .

"Gloria! What do I owe the pleasure of your visit?" I say as I open the door.

My diminutive neighbor is grasping a plate of brownies. Her gray hair is carefully coiffed as if she just came from the hairdresser. Her black slacks and red blouse are far too formal for a 10:00 a.m. coffee break on a Saturday.

"Maddie, dear, I baked these, and I don't want Charlie to eat all of them! His waistline doesn't need to expand any further. Thought I would share them with you and your new boyfriend." As she says this, she hustles inside the foyer and peers around the living room as if expecting to see Max lurking in the corner.

I force myself to suppress the laughter and ignore the boyfriend comment for now. "Let's go in the kitchen and I'll make a pot of coffee."

Miss Nosy Pants follows me into the kitchen, setting the overflowing plate of baked goods in the middle of the table and settling her small frame in one of the dining chairs. She's on high alert in case I'm hiding Max in the bedroom. Her beady eyes stare into the living room as if she's a sentry on watch for boyfriends trying to sneak out and not be caught. She's going to be very disappointed!

While the coffee brews I take a seat across from Gloria and wait for further questions. She doesn't disappoint.

"Charlie said a man mowed your yard last Saturday. Who was it?" The innocent timbre in her voice doesn't fool me. Gloria probably had *her nose* plastered to a window watching Max mow the yard.

"Oh, one of the Connor brothers stopped by and helped me." I feed her a tidbit even though she really wants me to spill all the beans.

After I fill our mugs, Gloria slides the brownies towards me. "Take one dear, they're my county fair purple ribbon award-winning recipe." I can almost see her chest swelling with pride.

Nodding, I grab one and take a bite of the gooey chocolate square. Savoring the taste sensation for several moments, I let silence fill the room. Gloria bakes a mean brownie.

"These are delicious, Gloria! I need to get the recipe."

After chewing her brownie, she replies, "I'll jot the recipe down when I get home and bring it right over. The secret is using two kinds of chocolate—milk and dark."

"Fascinating! I never would have thought to use two kinds," I say, stroking her ego even further.

Bringing our conversation back to the topic at hand, Gloria asks, "Which Connor brother?" A sly smile flits across her face then disappears.

I swallow my bite of brownie. "Max."

Gloria excitedly claps her hands. "I knew it! I told Charlie it was Max. He's grown into a fine-looking young man." She winks.

"I thought Charlie was the one spying on Max and me." I raise my eyebrow.

Gloria blushes then hands me another brownie. Clearly a diversionary tactic.

"Doug and Quinn were best friends in high school, and still are, for that matter. Sometimes Max hung round with them, but I haven't seen him for years. Did you know Quinn's wife Hailey lived with Amber while Doug was deployed to Afghanistan last year?" She sips on her coffee then continues. "The Connor boys were always so polite and friendly! How did you meet Max?" My wily companion casually sneaks that question in.

I grin. "He was one of my Calc 101 students several years ago. Max saw the story in the newspaper about the wrongful death settlement and stopped by my office a few weeks ago to offer his condolences." I blink my eyes furiously, holding back the tears that always threaten to fall when I mention Jack. "During our conversation, he volunteered to mow my yard." I pause several beats for effect and enunciate clearly, "We. Are. Not. Dating. His mowing the yard was just a friend helping a friend."

Gloria raises an eyebrow. I feel the heat of her gaze as she watches me take a sip of the hot brew. I almost crumble under her intent stare and nearly confess that I wish Max and I were dating. I manage to stay silent.

"So, you're seeing a younger man? I approve."

Did she not hear a word I just said? Do I need to hang up a sign that says "Maddie is not dating Max"?

I shrug and clear my throat. "He's only five years younger. Nothing really to be concerned about."

Do I hear myself? Suddenly the age difference doesn't matter.

Gloria takes a moment to finish her brownie. I try not to squirm under her intent look. When she's done sipping her coffee, she bangs the mug onto the table as if it's an exclamation mark to what she's going to say. Pointing a finger at me, she says, "You need to grasp the bull by the horns, Maddie! Don't let that nice young man slip away. Take it from an old coot like me, strike while the iron's hot!"

Although my neighbor drives me crazy with all her adages, her passionate delivery gets my attention. My eyes widen at the sight of the petite, grandmotherly neighbor telling me in no uncertain terms to pursue Max. Choking down my giggles, I reply. "I'll keep that in mind, Gloria."

She smirks.

Is this whole town filled with matchmakers?

~*~

During the last month since Hailey introduced herself, we've become good friends. She's a regular in yoga class, like I am. We chat before class and commiserate afterwards as to how much our muscles ache. This Monday Hailey arrives late, so we don't sit beside each other. But after class, Hailey waves and walks over with Amber Robinson in tow.

"Hey, Maddie, would you like to join us for coffee?"

My eyes widen at the welcome invite. "I'd love to!"

"Follow me, we're headed to Connor's Grove Bakery. Mary Sue texted that she just took some apple fritters out of the oven."

Well, let's speed right over! My mouth waters at the thought of the sweet treat.

When we arrive, I see why Hailey gets insider bakery information—the bakery is only two doors down from Connor Construction.

Delicious aromas of cinnamon, sugar, and baking bread assault my nose as we walk in. Bakery owner and fifty-something Mary Sue greets us exuberantly. "Hailey and friends! Welcome! Come over here to the display case and select your treat. The apple fritters are still warm." She's famous all over the tri-county area for her baked confections.

The three of us wander over to the bakery display case like moths drawn to a flame. I hope that I burned enough calories in yoga class because I'm having one of those giant fritters—they're bigger than Paul Bunyan's hand. I lick my lips in anticipation.

Hailey points to the fritters dripping with icing—messy to eat but oh so good. "I'll have one of those." She beams up at Mary Sue.

"Same!" Amber and I say in unison. We high-five at our identical responses.

Once we're sitting at one of the small café tables with our coffee and treats, Amber says, "I hear you're seeing Max Connor. The women of Connor's Grove will be extremely disappointed he's off the market."

Why do I feel like Gloria went straight home and enlisted the matchmaking help of Amber and Hailey? I've been bamboozled.

"Ah, well, we aren't formally dating. Just a few casual interactions." That explanation sounds lame even to me.

Hailey and Amber exchange a look that either says "she's kidding herself" or "these are the best apple fritters on the planet." I haven't learned how to fully interpret Hailey's expressions yet.

"Max would be the catch of the century," Amber adds. The corner of her mouth quirks up and she winks.

Hailey gives her friend a lopsided grin, then turns to me. "He's the best boss ever. And I can't believe how thoughtful he is. Just yesterday Max asked me how I'm feeling and whether I need to work part-time from home until the baby arrives."

What!? I haven't noticed a baby bump, so I excitedly clap my hands. "Congratulations! When are you due?"

Hailey blushes. "Next spring," she murmurs between bites.

I chew my delicious fritter, not quite knowing what to add. Silence falls between us as we sip the strong brew.

Max's PR person continues once she's devoured half her pastry, "Maddie, you'd be good for Max. He works too much. He's at our jobsites from dawn to dusk."

I catch myself before I snort. Both ladies are in full matchmaker mode and there's no stopping them. Time for a diversion.

"Would anyone like a refill? I'll go find the coffee pot." With that comment, I waltz up front, catching Mary Sue's eye.

"What ya need, honey?"

"Do you mind if I grab the coffee pot and refill our mugs?" I point to the carafe sitting on the warming burner behind the counter.

The older lady smiles. "Amber and Hailey trying to hook you up with Max Connor, eh?"

My forehead creases in shock that she listened to our whole conversation. But, why am I surprised? This is Connor's Grove.

Mary Sue puts her hand on my arm and gives me a saucy smile. "Don't let that one get away!" Then she turns, grabs the coffee pot, and trots over to our table.

I shrug and follow. There's a half-eaten fritter on my plate, and no amount of matchmaking will deter me from finishing it.

Chapter Eleven

Max

My hands grip the steering wheel as the day's frustrations play though my head. It's been a long, tiring twelve hours at one of our jobsites and I just want to get home.

Passing by the community college, I spy a familiar car in the parking lot. A beautiful professor is walking towards said vehicle. My day just got much better!

Turning into the parking lot, I pull up beside her. She glances over and smiles. I roll to a stop, lowering my window. "Why the late hour, Professor?"

She's toting that heavy bag and her purse. I want to jump out of the truck and help her, but it might make me look like an overeager puppy. So, I stay where I'm at.

Maddie sighs. "Everything that could go wrong today did. I'm just heading home after giving midterms."

She looks beat, but I throw out the suggestion anyway. "We can compare crappy days. How about something to eat?"

I can tell I've won her over when she giggles and nods. "Why not? I can grade these exams tomorrow morning."

My heart leaps at the prospect of spending time with her. "Follow me to Betty's Country Kitchen?" I nod my chin towards the highway. "It's just a few miles down the road."

"Sounds good!" Maddie climbs in her car and we head out.

The parking lot at the diner is deserted. We missed the rush that happened hours ago. Maddie meets me at the establishment's front door. I smile and hold it open for her.

The kitschy interior décor hasn't changed since this place opened in 1962. Despite being stuck in a time warp, the diner is neat and clean and serves the best homemade fare in the tri-county area.

"I haven't been here for years," my companion says as she stares around the eclectic room. Vintage memorabilia of all shapes and sizes grace the walls. An old rusty license plate. A black and white photograph of farmers harvesting hay. A well-used oxen yoke . . . The artifacts give a brief glimpse into local history, making the cluttered space somehow appealing.

A perky waitress seats us and hands out menus. "Hi! I'm Sandy. Welcome to Betty's Country Kitchen. What can I get ya to drink?"

I nod towards Maddie to order first.

"At this late hour, I think all I want is dessert."

A big smile crosses Sandy's face. "Betty makes the best desserts! We have pie, cobbler, and chocolate cake. What are you thinkin'?"

I chime in. "What kind of pie do you have?" My companion smiles and nods.

"Let me check what's still available." Sandy hustles off towards the bakery case at the front of the restaurant.

"My, oh my, do I love pie," Maddie says with a laugh.

I squint at her. "Line from a movie?"

She nods. "Do you know which one?"

The line sounds familiar, but it escapes me. "Nope. But I'm sure you'll tell me, Miss Trivia Champion."

She's a competitive trivia player. The whole class used to play Math Trivia on Fridays and no one could ever beat her.

Maddie nods. "*Michael.* The movie with John Travolta and Andie MacDowell."

"Right . . . He's an ugly, overweight angel in that one."

Sandy's return stops our conversation. "Cherry, peach, rhubarb, and chocolate cream," she says in one breathless statement. She then smiles with her pen poised to take our order.

"I'll have the chocolate cream," Maddie says.

65

Ah, I remember her addiction to chocolate. I file that away for future reference.

"I'll take the cherry."

We hand our menus back to our waitress. "Want coffee to go with that?"

"Yes, decaf," we reply in unison, then laugh.

After a few seconds of smiling at each other, Maddie breaks the silence. "So, tell me about your bad day and then I'll tell you about mine."

I sigh. Where do I begin? "I had a consultation with my high-profile client. His house is almost complete, and he wanted his new girlfriend to see it."

Maddie leans forward in the booth, shortening the distance between us, and says in almost a whisper, "The one you signed an NDA with?"

I smirk. "Yes, and I still can't tell you who he is . . ."

She shrugs as if that doesn't matter, but her eager look tells me otherwise.

"Today was the first time he brought Tiffany with him. And, well, she's quite a trip." I frown, a bad taste in my mouth at just the mention of that woman's name.

The professor grins and motions for me to continue.

"Tiffany's obvious 'physical assets' do not make up for her demanding personality." I make air quotes around physical assets because that is an understatement considering she must have had a boob job and face work. No one is born looking like that.

"What did she do?"

What didn't she do? "Nothing in the design or materials pleased her. She's into shiny surfaces, flashy fixtures, and shag carpet of all things! The mansion is going to look like a Las Vegas casino if we implement any of her changes. I walked away with a list of changes as long as my arm!"

Laughing, Maddie says, "Didn't Mr. Celebrity rein her in? It's his house."

"You'd never know he's a tough football player with how he deferred to the girlfriend on everything. Very frustrating."

Maddie's eyes widen. "You're building Brock Steele's new house?"

Oops. How did she guess? I shouldn't have mentioned his profession, but it could be any football player. I remain silent while I squirm in my seat and try to keep a poker-faced expression.

"Max, it was an easy guess! I had his little brother in class last semester, and he bragged about how his brother is building a mansion overlooking the river. Plus, Brock is the only pro football player who claims Connor's Grove as his hometown. I just put two and two together." Maddie reaches across the table and squeezes my hand. "Are you going to make all those changes?"

I shake my head. "Not right away. I'll drag my feet a few weeks in case he comes to his senses and breaks up with her."

She chuckles in agreement.

The waitress interrupts our discussion when she delivers the pie, pours two mugs of coffee, and leaves. We both eat in silence for a few minutes, savoring every bite. This was just the ticket after a day like today.

"This chocolate pie is to die for!" Maddie licks her lips and points her fork towards the sweet concoction. "By the way, I won't tell anyone," she adds and waggles her brows.

"You won't tell anyone the pie is fabulous or that I'm building a house for Mr. Steele?" I tease.

She rolls her eyes. "Eat your pie, Connor."

I smile, enjoying the cherry pie almost as much as watching Maddie eat the chocolate confection. Her little sighs of pleasure take my mind to another activity that might elicit those same sounds. I quickly push aside those thoughts.

Once the dessert plates are licked clean, we sip our coffee contentedly.

"Your turn. Tell me about Maddie's horrible day."

The professor smiles. "My Diffy Q exam was interrupted by a fire alarm."

I laugh. "The old 'I'm not ready for the test' trick, eh?"

She shakes her head. "No, I thought that at first, too. But they had a fire in the chemistry lab. We had to wait for sixty-five minutes while the fire department put out the fire, cleared all the smoke, and gave the all clear. Since this was a midterm, I couldn't delay it to another day. So, I stayed late giving my students the full three hours for the exam."

I remember the stress of midterms and how important it is to get the full period to finish. Nice touch for the professor to go the extra mile for her students. I wouldn't expect anything less from Maddie. "That's a long day. You look exhausted." My sympathetic look doesn't go unnoticed.

"Fortunately, my day just had a turn for the better!" She grins widely and nods towards her empty plate.

I raise my eyebrow. "Because of the chocolate pie?"

She giggles. "That and the company."

My heart flips. At least I compete with the pie.

Chapter Twelve

Maddie

Rebecca called this morning to see if I could watch her two-year-old son Logan for a few hours. My very pregnant sister-in-law needs to put up her feet for a while. Her husband is frantically working to get the addition completed on their home since the clock is ticking for the baby's arrival. I tell her I'd love to watch Logan—it'll be a fun way to spend my Friday, a day I have off from classes.

When I pull up at my in-laws' house, there's a flurry of activity going on. Pickup trucks are parked everywhere, lumber is stacked beside the garage, and when I step out of the car, I hear power tools rumbling from the backyard. Becca wasn't kidding about the push to get the new addition on the house finished.

Eight-months-pregnant Becca answers the door, her stomach extending out in front of her such that I can barely get my arms around her for a hug. She waddles back towards the living room and I follow.

"Sorry for the mess," she says as she sighs and flops back on the sofa. Toys are strewn around the living room, and a plate with a half-eaten bagel sits on the coffee table along with two empty coffee mugs. Stacks of magazines are vying for the only remaining space on the end table, along with two Dr. Pepper cans and an empty package of Oreos. Becca must also be suffering from the munchies.

Logan pops up from playing with his trucks, running to me and hugging my legs. "Auntie Maddie!"

I kneel and hug him back. He's still in his PJs and his hair is a curly mess, as if a comb hasn't touched his head for days, but his sweet smile brings joy to my heart. It's obvious that Rebecca hasn't been feeling well for quite some time. I'll get this place cleaned up in no time.

"Logan let's go play in your room while Mommy takes a nap. Okay?"

He smiles, pulling on my hand towards his bedroom.

I resist his pull for a moment as I nod at Rebecca. "Do you need anything other than some peace and quiet? Can I help you to your bed?"

She smiles. "I think I'll stay right here. I'm too tired to move, and the sofa is only fifteen steps to the bathroom, which I need to visit on a regular basis."

A little pang of jealousy hits. Maybe it's silly to be jealous of having to pee all the time. But I've never gotten to experience the joys or discomforts of a baby growing inside me. Jack and I both wanted children in the worst way, but I was never able to conceive. It's a well-kept secret because Jack and I never mentioned it to anyone. We had a hard time facing the fact ourselves.

I'm used to swallowing the jealousy, so I just chuckle and wave for her to take her seat. Once Becca is settled on the couch with the colorful afghan her mom made placed over her swollen feet, the toddler and I walk back to his bedroom.

Logan's room is even messier than the living room. I show Logan how to put toys back into the big crate at the end of his bed. We make a game out of it while I make his bed. The cute comforter features several different types of spaceships floating in space. Logan toddles over holding a giant stuffed Olaf and places him on the bed. *Frozen* meets NASA. I giggle at the sight.

Finding a clean pair of shorts and a T-shirt in one of his drawers, I change Logan out of his pajamas. He wants to play with his Duplo blocks—he calls them Legos—so we do that. The bigger blocks fit his tiny hands, and he's quite adept at building with them.

Soon he has a tower constructed and I'm working on a blocky looking dragon.

Crash!

The loud noise from the backyard gets my attention. I stand to peek out the back window, looking directly at the construction site. Men of all shapes and sizes are hammering, sawing, and putting up the new addition. I spot one guy who stands out from the rest— Max.

My eyes widen because he's removed his T-shirt and is helping frame walls. His naked chest glistens in the sun, making my mouth water. The temps are over 90 degrees, so I don't blame him and the others who have also removed their sweaty shirts. Max has, by far, the sexiest chest of everyone. I chuckle when I see my brother-in-law standing beside Max because Jim looks like a chubby teddy bear, where Max looks like Adonis.

I'm not sure how long I stand and watch the magnificent sight. A small hand tugs at my shorts. "Auntie Maddie, I'm hungry."

"Let's go get something to eat," I say as I reluctantly pull my gaze from the backyard.

Heading into the kitchen with Logan, we bump into Rebecca returning from the powder room. She shakes her head and giggles. "The baby is sitting right on my bladder. I swear I have to use the bathroom every ten minutes!"

I rub her back. "Want some lunch? Logan's hungry, so I'm going to fix something for him."

"Sure," she says, moving slowly behind us, her huge stomach making her gait very awkward. I help settle her into one of the padded chairs at the dining table. From this vantage point we can see the mass of men working on the addition.

Rebecca raises an eyebrow and nods towards the rear window. "The construction guys have been here since six this morning. Jim wants the addition enclosed by Monday. It looks like they brought an army to help!"

I smile, remaining silent as I get out sandwich fixings from the fridge.

"How did the lunch with Max Connor go?" Her words hang between us because I've never given her an update on the date or the fact that he mowed my yard last weekend.

Turning with packages of turkey and cheddar cheese in my hands, I walk to the island. "He mowed my yard and we went out for lunch once. While it was nice, I still feel like I need some more time to get over Jack." My lips wobble and my voice cracks.

Becca clucks her tongue like a disapproving mother hen. "Sweetie, you need to keep seeing him. He's a catch! In fact, if my eyes are correct, he's the sexiest man out there. Especially with that shirt off." She smirks when she says it.

I feel my neck and cheeks heating. "I hadn't noticed."

She emits a huge belly laugh. It's particularly impressive with her extra girth, although I'm a little nervous that the laughter may set off premature labor. "I peeked in while you were playing in Logan's room, and someone was glued to the window."

Caught in the act. I give her an embarrassed grin. "Maybe I did watch for a few minutes."

Our discussion is interrupted when Jim comes bounding in the back door. Logan runs over, and his dad picks him up, giving him a loud smooch on the cheek. "How's my boy?"

Logan squeals while Jim tosses him up and down a few times.

My brother-in-law looks over at me. "Nice to see you, Maddie. Thanks for helping. Poor Becca hasn't been feeling very good and I'm caught up in trying to get this addition done. We're so grateful for your help." He walks over to his pregnant wife, gently kissing her on the top of her head.

72

"I was delighted Becca called. You know I'm always happy to help. When Logan takes his nap, I'll get things tidied up a bit."

He smiles, reminding me so much of Jack that I suck in my breath.

"Can you bring out some sodas and lemonade for the guys?" He nods towards the backyard. "They're all working over lunch, so I want to give them something."

"We have lots of meat and cheese, they can fix sandwiches," Rebecca adds.

I shoo Jim back outside. "I'll set up a feast on the back patio: drinks and food. Let me get Becca and Logan fed first."

Jim smiles as he walks out the back door.

I look sternly at my sweet sister-in-law. "Is this a setup to get Max and me together? I'm supposed to swoon over his naked chest?"

She giggles. "Is it working?"

I roll my eyes as I return to fixing lunch.

Chapter Thirteen

Max

Seeing Maddie holding Jim and Becca's little boy makes my heart tingle. Logan is pulling her hair while she laughs. He puts his tiny hands up to her cheeks, turning her eyes toward him. "Auntie Maddie, I want some chips."

She's fixed everyone a lunch feast on the back patio—sandwiches, chips, cookies, and drinks all spread out before us. Moving over to the table, she gets out a paper plate, puts several chips on it, and sits Logan at the picnic table holding the food. "Sit here and eat your chips. Do you want some lemonade?"

He shakes his head while placing chips into his mouth as quickly as possible. Maddie looks over his head, catching my eyes. We exchange sappy grins. I can't keep my eyes off her.

Jim goes inside to be with Becca for a few minutes. That leaves me and my crew on the patio with Maddie and Logan. Several of my guys are flirting with her, making me a little jealous. I try to push down the green monster because my crew doesn't know Maddie and I are a thing. *At least, I think we're a thing.* Jim introduced her as his sister-in-law and a professor at the local college, so the topic appears to be "guess what subject the pretty lady teaches."

Big Bob says in his booming voice, "I bet you teach history. You look like a history buff."

Maddie grins. "That's my least favorite subject! Try again." Everyone groans.

Shorty Carlson chimes in, "Psychology. You handle Logan like a pro." He then winks at the little boy who's quietly eating his chips.

Maddie giggles and shakes her head. "That's called being an aunt . . . Think numbers."

Tom adds "Accounting!" smiling as if he's won the grand prize.

Logan even gets in on the action, "Legos!" His cute, high-pitched baby voice makes everyone laugh.

Maddie tickles his curly head. "That's a great guess Logan, but I only play Legos with you."

He smiles proudly at her remark.

Finally, I add to the fray. "She was my professor when I went there."

The guys' eyes widen. "No kidding, boss," Tom says. "She was your professor?"

"Basket weaving!" Shorty shouts out in triumph. The expression on his face changes to a cringe once he realizes that he accidently insulted Maddie while taking a dig at me. "Sorry ma'am, I didn't mean anything against you by that comment." He blushes beet red, matching his T-shirt. You can't tell where his shirt ends and his neck begins.

The professor just laughs. Logan claps.

After a few minutes quietly eating their sandwiches, Tom says, "Calculus. You taught the boss that highbrow math stuff."

"Bing. Bing. Bing!" I say as Maddie grins.

Bob and Shorty throw a handful of chips at Tom for guessing the correct answer. The men are obviously impressed by Maddie's profession because they are polite and well behaved for the remainder of the meal. Shorty even comments that his son is taking algebra in high school and it makes Shorty's head hurt just thinking about it. Heads nod in agreement around the table.

The plate of cookies disappears, and the party breaks up once we finish most of the food. My crew politely thanks Maddie as they shuffle back to the construction zone, the hot weather making them lethargic and not anxious to return to the back-breaking work.

"Max, I'll leave the sodas out here in the cooler, along with the lemonade. Please tell your guys to take as much as they want. I know it's hot out here." When Maddie says that, she glances at my naked chest, a blush crossing her cheeks.

She's not immune to my body. Good to know.

I walk into her personal space, whispering in her ear, "You look beautiful despite the heat. I especially like the ponytail." I give her ponytail a quick tug. She usually wears her hair in a professional-looking bun or hanging lose. The ponytail makes her look casual and carefree.

We stand there looking into each other's eyes for what feels like minutes but is probably only seconds. I breathe in her intoxicating scent of vanilla and peaches. It must be the shampoo or body wash she uses because she always smells like this. Hopefully I smell better than sweat and sawdust, but I doubt it.

Jim walks through the backdoor and onto the patio, breaking up our staring fest. I back up a couple of steps while Jim ruffles his son's hair and steals a chip off his plate. A pink blush crawls up Maddie's neck and across her cheeks.

"Are you ready to get back to work?" Jim asks me. From his teasing tone, he noticed the staring match I was having with his sister-in-law.

I clear my throat. "Ready when you are."

As we walk to the backyard, I look over my shoulder. Maddie's still gazing at me. Her look tells me that it's just a matter of time before she agrees to another date. I grin, thankful that the hot weather forced me to remove my sweaty shirt.

Chapter Fourteen

Maddie

Max is rapidly wearing down my resistance. Whew! Does that man ever look good without a shirt. Now I wish he would have gotten more overheated while mowing my yard. He's definitely swoon-worthy, but it's his funny texts, photos, and another round of flowers that are winning me over. He's so attuned to what I like—this time the flowers he sent are a pot of orange-colored mums to plant in my yard. With autumn approaching, that's a perfect gift.

At the same time, Professor Bolton has stepped up his game trying to get me to go out on a date with him. He pops into my office several times during the day to gab about our colleagues or students. I didn't realize until recently what a gossip William is. Sometimes during the conversation, he neatly works in a mention of going out to dinner. So far I've had actual conflicts and haven't had to analyze too closely why that didn't disappoint me more.

It's exhausting pondering what to do with two men pursuing me. They're both slowly chipping away at the wall I've built around my heart and my resistance to dating. I stew about the William-Max conundrum every night when I go to bed and every morning when I wake up. My brain tells me that the prudent choice is William. He's attractive in a nerdy professor sort of way. We have common interests, although if I'm honest, those narrow down to math and the community college. Most of all he's the safe choice—he doesn't make my palms sweat or my heart palpitate.

On the other hand, my heart wants Max. No amount of arguing with it makes any difference. Max makes my stomach flip-flop, my arm tingle when he touches me, and my rapid heartbeat says, "Choose him! Choose him!" He's attractive in a mouth-watering, knee-weakening way. Our common interests so far are math word problems, yardwork, and pie. But, hey, we've only just scratched the surface! The truth is, Max is a danger to my comfortable life, which scares me to death.

When Professor Bolton asked me for the umpteenth time during one of our lunches to go to dinner and a movie with him, my brain and my mouth reluctantly replied, "Sure, that sounds fun." Did I finally agree because I want to go out with him or because I'm getting tired of him asking? Right after the words slipped through my lips, my heart argued, "You're a fool! You know you really want Max."

Sigh. If only my heart would shut up and let me enjoy the date with William. During my thirty-two years, I don't have any experience with multiple men pursuing me. I tell myself that I shouldn't fall for the first guy who comes along, even if he is sexy Mr. Connor. I rationalize that accepting the dinner and movie date with William will be a good test to see whether my comfortable feelings for the professor win over my heart-pounding infatuation with the hunky builder.

Ding! Dong!

I jump even though I'm expecting him. Walking to the door, I open it to a smiling William standing on the front porch holding a bouquet of red roses. Um . . . It strikes me that the only man who knows what type of flowers I like is Max.

"Please come in!" I usher him into the foyer.

He hands me the flowers with a flourish as if he's giving me gold. "Beautiful flowers for a beautiful lady." He looks like he's going to bow but restrains himself.

I smile, somehow say the right gushy thing about the roses, then walk into the kitchen to put them in a vase. The only vase handy is the gorgeous cut-crystal one Max gave me. I shake my head at the irony.

Fibi is sniffing William's shoe when I return. Professor Bolton looks a little uncomfortable around my dog, and he's certainly not petting the border collie with relish like Max did.

"Fibi, come here. Time to go to your bed." I point to his bed in the corner and my well-behaved dog obeys. "Don't you like dogs?" I ask.

"I'm allergic to them, so I try never to pet one."

Um . . . that comment is a game changer. Too bad I can't back out of this date now!

I grab my purse and a light wrap, and we walk to William's silver sedan. He helps me inside and then settles into the driver's seat.

"I made reservations at Benny's Steakhouse. Hope that's okay?"

Um . . . last time I was there the steak was tough as leather, but I don't mention that. "Sure, that sounds good." We exchange smiles, although mine's fake.

On the drive over, we discuss some of our mutual students. If I'm honest with myself, that's all we ever seem to talk about. That or William's heavy class workload, which he complains about incessantly. When Max complained about the high-profile client's girlfriend, it rolled right off my back. His grumbling was funny and didn't come off as whining like William's does.

Dinner is okay. I opt for the salmon instead of steak this time and it's done to perfection. The baked potato is a little soggy, and the side vegetable is broccoli that they forgot to cook. I crunch through one stalk and leave the rest on my plate.

William is sawing through his ribeye. "Have you created the Diffy Q final exam yet? I'd be happy to review it and make suggestions once you have it done."

Um . . . Is William suddenly the head of the Math Department? I work to suppress the glower that I want to give him. "Oh, thanks, but I haven't made it up yet. Plus, you're too busy with all your workload." I wave my hand in a dismissive motion, hoping he'll get the hint.

William smirks. "It is your first time teaching the class. Thought you might need a little mentoring."

My neck heats and I choke back the words I really want to say: *I don't need any help developing a final exam, you pompous butt!* Instead, I politely shake my head and decline his offer.

I excuse myself to the ladies room to settle my anger. Pacing in the tiny restroom helps work off a little of the steam. How have I had so many lunches with this guy and just shaken off his condescending remarks? Probably since those conversations weren't a date but just two colleagues conversing. I was happy to ignore William's flaws, which are coming out loud and clear tonight. *Maybe I should develop a sudden migraine and ask to go home?* I square my shoulders. There won't be much talking during the movie, so I decide to just get it over with and then never date this man again.

Looking in the cracked mirror beside the sink, I smile, consoling myself that the silver lining from this awful attempt to reenter the dating scene, is that Max Connor wins hands down. No more doubts on my part. I can't wait to let Max know I'm ready to start dating him!

William pays the bill and we drive over to the MetroPlex in Hudson. It's the closest movie theatre to Connor's Grove that shows first run movies. I suggest we go to one of the Marvel movies. I've been looking forward to this one, and I know there will be a lot of action and no nude scenes. Williams whines that he prefers something more highbrow but he capitulates to my suggestion.

We stand in the long line waiting to buy our tickets. It's Friday night, so there's a huge crowd to see the movie still in its first week since opening. I glance down the long row of loitering people and do a double take when I spot Hailey and Quinn. Max jogs up to join them and they all laugh. My heart sinks like a rock to my toes. I try to sneak behind William, who's oblivious to my plight. He gives me a "what are you doing" glare and moves so I'm standing beside him.

Never in a million years did I think I would see Max at the theater. Yet here he is in the flesh. I wish the ground would swallow me up. How is this going to look? I tell Max that I need more time and refuse to date him, but then I go on a date with William? Groaning internally, I can only pray that none of the Connors spot me.

A group of teenagers come up behind William and me. They're making a lot of noise and one of them keeps horsing around with his skateboard. It's annoying everyone standing nearby. The boy with the skateboard crashes it against the curb with a loud crash. All eyes in the line swivel towards him.

I stand stock still, but Hailey spots me, yelling my name and waving. Where's my cloaking device? Why didn't I wear a disguise? Panic fills my heart knowing I've screwed up big time. After a few beats, I look up and wave back, trying to act casual. I want to shout "I'm here with a colleague, no biggie" but the lie would be difficult to pull off, especially when William suddenly decides to hold my hand.

The Connor trio all realize at the same instant that I'm here with a date. William's standing awfully close to me, talking at me animatedly while I try to no avail to dislodge my hand from his. The welcoming expression on all their faces evaporates before my eyes.

After a few beats, I sneak a peek directly at Max. Initially his expression is one of confusion. Who can blame him, since I told him I wasn't ready to date *anyone*? Once he takes in the scene of William standing in my personal space and holding my hand, his glare meets my eyes as his ocean blue orbs turn ice cold. His expression looks like a dark, thunderous cloud. He doesn't acknowledge me but rather turns towards Quinn and Hailey, who obviously try to smooth over the situation with conversation.

Hailey glances back at me in confusion, then she also turns her back to me. The friendship we've developed during yoga class blows up in my face. Tears well up in my eyes, and I feel like something slammed into my chest, making it difficult to breathe and swallow. William keeps talking as if nothing happened. I nod in the correct spots but am not listening to a thing he's saying.

Eventually the line moves, we get our tickets, and go into the theater. I pull William towards the opposite entrance from where I saw the Connors enter and pray that we don't run into them face-to-face. Out of the corner of my eye I see them sitting towards the front rows, so I tell William I love watching movies from the back row. He looks at me like I'm ridiculous, but thankfully he doesn't complain.

We settle into our seats; the room goes dark and I hope that two hours of superheroes saving the planet will be a good diversion. But I can't concentrate on the movie. All I can think about are those glacial blue eyes glaring at me. I feel sick that I didn't think this date with William through better. The excuses I gave Max now just look like an excuse not to date *him*. I wouldn't be surprised if he never believes what I say or trusts me again. My heart is broken. How can I win him back?

Chapter Fifteen

Max

My life's in meltdown since seeing Maddie with another man. Tonight's another night of meeting my buddies at Johnson's Pub and trying to make myself forget the woman of my dreams. Nothing numbs the pain from the blow to my heart.

Matt, Mike, and I were buddies in high school, and I can't say that either of them has matured much since then. We were known as the 3 M's; on the football team together, attending the best keggers together, and basically skating through school with barely passing grades. Part of the reason I started out at the community college is my grades weren't good enough to get into a university. I cringe at the old me, and yet here I am—being the old high school Max again.

I cough at the cigarette smoke surrounding the pool table in the back corner of the bar. It's created a blue fog floating around the room, highlighting all the dust particles swirling in its haze. Not a healthy environment. No worries. I probably have enough alcohol in my system to kill off even the most virulent disease. Matt and Mike are nowhere in sight, wisely abandoning me hours ago. They're tucked into their beds while I'm still at this stinky tavern.

"Babe, are you ever going to take that shot?" The buxom blonde I've been hanging around with all night saunters up to me, rubbing her hands on my biceps. Her low-cut tank top leaves very little to the imagination and I'm just waiting for her girls to spill out completely.

I move away from her, pull back the cue stick, and scatter the billiard balls around the table. Hitting them hard enough to break up the pack but not with enough finesse to put any in the pocket. *Oh darn.*

She laughs as she picks up her cue stick. Her throaty voice makes me wonder if she's a smoker. Maybe she's the one creating the blue fog; my booze-addled brain hadn't noticed.

Bending over the table right in front of me, she wiggles her butt in the tight blue jeans. I watch even though I'm disinterested. She hits a ball into the pocket, giggling up at me, then she moves to the next shot. I lean against my cue stick, taking a slow sip of my beer. The blonde waltzes over, takes the beer from my hand and takes a big gulp. *So now we're sharing drinks? I don't think so.*

When she hands the beer mug back to me, I place it on a nearby table. The red lipstick stain on the rim makes me sick to my stomach.

After the blonde runs the table, she plasters herself against my body. "Come on honey bear, let's go back to my place." I stare down at her. She isn't without certain assets that a guy might find interesting, alluring, and sexy.

Do I want to go back to her place? Part of my brain says "yes," that act will get Maddie out of my system once and for all. The other part of my brain vehemently says "no." I've resisted this urge since seeing the professor on a date with another man, so why give in now? Even though Bambi or Barbie or whatever her name is seems very willing, it isn't my style to pick up women at a bar and spend the night with them. I've never done that before.

She sees my hesitation, so she pulls me in for a sloppy kiss. I quickly pull back. This needs to end. Right. Now.

"Big Max, what's wrong?" she coos at up at me, batting her fake eyelashes and pouting her red, Botox-enhanced lips.

"I need a bathroom break," I say as I gently extract her arms from around me and walk off towards the back hallway where the restrooms are located. Once I'm out of her range of vision, I go to the end of the hall and exit through the back door. The alley reeks of vomit and garbage, but I take a big breath anyway to rid my lungs of the cigarette smoke. I almost puke in the process.

Clearing my head, I turn and walk towards 5th Street. It's only three blocks to my office where I can spend the night. I turn my head several times, glancing back over my shoulder to make sure no one's following me, namely the voluptuous blonde. I'm such a chicken ducking out like that, but I wasn't going home with her. No. Way.

I arrive, flop onto the uncomfortable futon in the back room, and toss and turn all night. This pattern has been repeating itself nightly since I saw Maddie with that other guy. I sleep late every morning as if I can't bear for another day without Maddie to begin. Only Hailey's office management keeps the business running smoothly. She's even helping direct my crews at jobsites while I sleep until noon. This is what my life has become. I'm a sad, pathetic mess, and I don't like myself anymore.

My heart is fractured, splintered into a million pieces such that I may not be able to put it back together. Maddie asked for time, so I honored her request. Then she dates one of her colleagues behind my back?! They deserve each other—two math nerds. He looked like a pompous type of guy. All that hand gesturing and talking. Maddie looked like she wanted to crawl in a hole. Good—I hope she feels guilty for a long time.

I stop the ranting in my brain. The truth is I miss her terribly. Several times a day I think of something to text her and have to stop myself from doing so. My brain reminds me that I'm furious with her. My heart reminds me that down deep inside, I still love her.

~*~

"Up and at 'em!"

The loud voice rings in my head, making it hurt like I've been hit with a board. I struggle to sit up, cracking my eyes open a millimeter. "What?!!" I croak out when I see Quinn and Jacob staring at me. They're grinning at my obvious pain.

"We're taking you someplace this morning! Let's get going!" Quinn's overly cheerful voice makes me grumpier.

"I don't want to go anywhere," I say, then try to huddle back under the blanket on the lumpy futon.

"This is an intervention, Brother. You have no choice," little brother Jacob says with such a determined look my eyes widen. Where has this version of Jacob been at recent family gatherings? He's seemed so aloof lately, caught up in his big city advertising job, and not engaged with family happenings.

"Wait! This is Saturday. I don't need to be anywhere," I say with a yawn as I try to lie back down.

Quinn grabs my arm. "Brother, you're coming with me and Jacob. Go freshen up or we'll be late."

Complaining loudly, I drag myself to the office bathroom to wash some of the pub dirt off. I find a new Connor Construction T-shirt in Hailey's desk and put it on. My blue jeans from the previous day will have to do. Mom didn't say anything about a family get-together, so where are we going?

My brothers look up as I reenter the office. My head hurts, but the ibuprofen I took should take effect soon.

"You look a little better than a wet dog now," Jacob says as we walk out the door.

"At least you don't smell like a pub anymore," Quinn adds. Both brothers laugh at my expense.

I shield my eyes from the glaring sun. My headache isn't getting any better.

We get in Quinn's massive pickup and drive away. Did Jacob say something about an intervention? My brain finally catches up.

~*~

Connor's Grove town hall is hopping for a Saturday morning. Cars fill the parking lot and Quinn takes the last open spot. He turns off the engine and both my brothers turn to look at me huddling in the backseat. I sit up straighter at their serious expressions.

Jacob talks first. "Max, this is a kick-off meeting for Big Brothers Big Sisters of Connor's Grove. I belong to the Minneapolis chapter. One of our goals is to open chapters in smaller communities to address the needs of at-risk kids all over. Provide an opportunity for them to have a big brother or big sister mentor in their lives. Quinn and I are sponsoring this chapter and we want you to help us. Are you in?"

My eyes widen. Jacob never mentioned this organization or his involvement in it. Very impressive. Maybe he hasn't just been living it up in the big city rather than attending family gatherings.

I nod. Quinn and Jacob exchange a look I can't decipher, then get out of the truck. I follow suit.

We go to a large meeting room in the historic building. Jacob greets a couple guys who are apparently also members of the Minneapolis organization and here to help with the kickoff. Many fellow Connor's Grove businessmen are milling around, drinking coffee and talking. Quinn waves to John and Erma Vandervoldt who own the lumberyard in town. Their son Erik is with them, along with his wife Amy. Quinn helped them adopt a baby boy from Guatemala last year. My work neighbor Mary Sue from the bakery smiles and waves at me across the sea of heads.

Mr. Chen walks up, slapping Quinn on the back. He owns the tattoo shop in the strip mall where Quinn has his law office. "I hear congratulations are in order! I saw Hailey the other day and she told me about the baby," he says with a smile and a wink.

Quinn laughs. "Duck is going to have a sibling soon. How do you think he'll like that?" Duck is the Chesapeake Bay Retriever that Mr. Chen gave to Hailey and Quinn as a wedding present. They had already almost adopted the dog, so putting the bow on was just a formality.

The two men converse for a few minutes while I survey the room. My framing foreman Luke Anderson is over by the cookies chatting with Uncle Bob—former owner of Connor Construction. The two men wave at me and I wave back.

My younger brother takes charge of the meeting, and I can't help but beam with pride. "Good morning! I'd like to call this meeting to order. Please take a seat and we'll get started."

Once everyone is settled in their seats, Jacob continues. "As you probably already know, the Big Brothers Big Sisters organization's goal is for all young people to achieve their full potential. We are the nation's largest volunteer mentoring network. Today I'll explain what is expected from a mentor and the vetting process. Once you're vetted, the organization will provide each of you who want to volunteer with the name of a child from the local Connor's Grove area to mentor. Additional materials are available at the back of the room." Heads turn to the table where Jacob is pointing to.

Quinn smiles over at me. I'm in awe of my little brother and his involvement in this organization. Also, I'm embarrassed that I didn't join a group like this sooner. Focusing on helping a child who needs a positive force in their life might help me turn my life back around and forget the sexy professor. It's just what I need!

Chapter Sixteen

Maddie

Max ignores all my texts and phone calls. I've tried for two weeks to get him to talk to me with no luck. I gave him some time to cool off, so today I'm taking the bull by the horns, as Gloria would say. I'll force Hailey to talk to me after yoga class. She's been frosty and avoiding me since the movie date disaster. I'll appeal to her desire to see Max and me together. I need her advice on how to get his attention.

The yoga instructor leads a brutal workout this morning. I'm at my usual spot in the back of the room, sweat pouring off my body and my legs barely able to hold my weight. Hailey's up front beside Amber.

When the class starts breaking up, I rush to the front of the room so Hailey can't get away without me speaking to her. "Hailey, can I talk to you?"

Amber and Hailey turn to face me. Amber's expression isn't much friendlier than Hailey's. They're both obviously in Camp Max. I have no supporters in Camp Maddie.

Hailey leans in and whispers something to Amber. Her friend nods, then walks away. Turning towards me, Hailey crosses her arms over her chest. Her body language is not encouraging.

I clear my throat and pace back and forth, uncomfortable having this discussion in front of other yoga students, but the classroom is emptying quickly so I'm out of excuses. "I know you're mad at me and I understand that. Max didn't deserve me dating someone else behind his back. I had what I felt were legitimate reasons for doing what I did, but now I realize I was an idiot. I never intended to hurt him. I want to win Max back, but he won't take any of my phone calls or respond to any of my texts. What can I do?"

The desperation in my voice causes Hailey's expression to soften a little. "Do you truly care for him? Are you ready to give 100 percent to a relationship with him?"

I feel the ghost of a smile form on my face after her passionate comeback. Max has some pretty great friends and family to rely on.

"Yes, I'm ready. I'd explain everything to Max if he'd talk to me . . ." My voice trails off in embarrassment. Blowing out a breath in frustration, I continue. "Do you know his schedule? Could I drop in at Connor Construction and catch him today?"

Hailey's frosty expression thaws even further. "Yeah, he'll be in his office at two today. But, if you break his heart again, I'll beat you with my yoga mat!" Her half smile tells me that's a false threat.

I reach over and squeeze her arm. "I'll be there!"

~*~

Turning into the parking lot, I spot Max's truck. The breath I've been holding swooshes out. At least he's here. My fingers are crossed and I'm praying he'll talk to me.

It took me forty-five minutes to get ready. I tried on several outfits before I decided on my jet-black jeans and a sky-blue crop top that shows off my figure without looking sleezy. The color reminds me of Max's eyes. A pair of wedge sandals give the outfit a sexy look. At least, I hope Max thinks so.

The bells above the door jingle as I walk in. Thankfully Hailey's at her desk, peering at her computer and sipping what looks like 7 Up. A few saltine crackers sit beside her keyboard. A pang goes through my heart at the implications. She'd been looking a little green at yoga class. I guess I'm just bound to be surrounded by happily pregnant women.

I swallow the bitter thought and focus on why I'm here. As I approach the desk, Hailey looks up and smiles. *At least one Connor is happy to see me.* She stands. "Let me go tell Max you're here. He was on a call with some clients a few minutes ago. He doesn't know you're coming."

Smart move, keeping Max in the dark, otherwise I'm sure he would be hightailing it to a jobsite right now.

I nod, continuing to stand while I wait. The office is small but well organized. With the many stacks of paper on Hailey's desk, it looks like they're busy.

I hear muffled voices after Hailey disappears inside the back room, clicking the door shut behind her. Whatever they're saying is taking several minutes. My heart plummets. Is he going to refuse to see me?

Hailey re-appears. "You can go in now." She nods towards the door and gives me an encouraging smile.

As soon as I enter Max's office, Hailey pulls the door shut behind me. The click echoes loudly in the room and my palms start to sweat.

Max is sitting behind his massive desk. Papers and what looks to be blueprints are stacked everywhere on its surface. He looks wonderful in his blue button-down collar shirt that matches his eyes, and the khaki pants add a professional touch. I gulp and keep walking towards the two chairs in front of his desk. Max doesn't move a muscle.

"May I sit down?" I motion towards the left chair.

"I only have a few minutes, Madeleine, but go ahead." The tone of his voice is not encouraging. The use of my formal first name speaks volumes—as if we can no longer even be friends. I almost turn around and run out, but I force myself to sit down in the chair instead.

We stare at each other for several moments. He finally points his finger at the watch strapped to his wrist as if to say *Get on with it*.

I launch into my prepared speech. Hopefully he'll listen. "I met Jack in college when I was nineteen. He was twenty-three, and I thought it was wonderful to have an upper classman notice me. Going to college was my first time away from home. I was a lonely and scared freshman, so Jack's friendship meant a lot."

Max is listening and hasn't cut me off yet, so I take a quick breath and plow on.

"We were both in Ancient History together. Jack needed two more social studies credits in order to graduate, so he was the lone senior in the freshman class. I sat next to him on the first day of class, spilling the contents of my backpack all over the floor at his feet. He helped me pick everything up and introduced himself."

A small smile crosses Max's face when I mention my clumsiness. Taking that as a positive sign, I keep going.

"We started dating, and by the end of the semester, we were engaged. Jack was the first and only boy I'd ever dated. I wouldn't call our match a passionate one, but rather two friends who learned to love each other. Don't get me wrong, I loved Jack with all my heart, but he didn't give me heart palpitations like you do."

Max raises an eyebrow.

I'm laying open my soul to him, not holding anything back. "We got married after Jack graduated. He supported me as I finished my undergraduate degree and also through grad school. He was my rock when I thought I couldn't make it. I owe my becoming a math professor to Jack." Pausing to clear my throat, I blink furiously to hold back the tears that are threatening to fall. I knew this was going to be hard, but talking about my husband is much more difficult than I imagined. I thought that since I'd practiced the speech so many times I'd be able to do it without falling apart. Guess I was wrong. I take a deep breath and keep going.

"Once I graduated with my masters, we moved back to Connor's Grove. Jack got a job working as a lineman for Minnesota Power. I got the teaching job at the community college. A few years later, we bought the house and fixed it up. Fibi and I got involved in Agility competitions at Jack's urging and support. We had seven lovely years together before Jack's accident. The day he died was one of the worst days of my life." I close my eyes and take a big breath. It's almost impossible for me to talk about the specifics of Jack's death even after almost two years. My lips wobble.

I don't look at Max because now I know I'll start to cry, so I just keep talking, focusing on the brown rug under my feet and my hands clasped in my lap.

Even though I know Max read about the wrongful death lawsuit in the newspaper, I feel compelled to share this information—and make it clear that my husband didn't make a careless mistake. "Jack was electrocuted while trying to repair a downed power line. One of the assistants on the job mistakenly thought the power was off. The instant Jack touched it, he was gone. His supervisor came to the house and told me. I'll never forget all the details of that day, as if it's frozen in my mind. I was making Jack's favorite meal at the time the doorbell rang. I can't ever cook lasagna again for as long as I live . . ." My voice cracks.

Max stands and walks over to sit in the chair next to me. He takes my hand. A few tears roll down my cheeks, but I bravely meet his eyes. "Max, I've never been with any man other than Jack. I went on the date with William because I wanted to be sure about my feelings. I know that sounds crazy, but I wanted to know that you're the one and that I didn't just jump at a chance with the first guy who paid me any attention since my husband's death."

He nods and squeezes my hand. His beautiful blue eyes meet mine and I see sympathy reflected back at me. I look back down at my hands and continue. If I look up, I'll break down even further.

"The date with William was a disaster, as you may have noticed. Before we saw you, I was ready to bail and go home. At the restaurant I hid in the bathroom for fifteen minutes, wondering if I should feign a migraine so he'd take me home. But I decided to see the date to the end because how much more could he talk about himself during a movie?"

I finally look up and stare Max straight in the eye. His soft smile is encouraging. My heart soars with hope that he's understanding what I'm trying to explain. "I'm so sorry I hurt you. I overthink everything, just like I did about our relationship. At first, I didn't think I was ready to let Jack go. I felt like I would be cheating on my husband." I bite my lip at that confession. Max nods.

"When I finally got past that obstacle in my mind, I decided I needed to be sure you're the one. When William asked me out, it seemed like a good opportunity to confirm my feelings for you or for him. I'm not attracted to William so much as he's a safe choice. A comfortable relationship without a lot passion. You see, Max, I'm terrified about how you make me feel."

He stands, pulling me into his arms. "I understand Maddie," he says in his rumbly voice, full of emotion.

Max's words break the fragile dam holding back my tears. I put my arms around his waist and sob uncontrollably for several minutes. He rubs my back saying, "It's okay Maddie. Let it out."

Eventually I run out of tears. The mascara that I painstakingly applied has probably run all over my face. But when I look up at Max, his smile lights up his face. My chin rests on his soaked shirt. I put my hand up to his cheek, rubbing his stubbly beard, which is fuller than before, as if he doesn't have the time or inclination to keep it trimmed anymore. *Did seeing me with William put him in a tailspin?*

He leans in, giving me a gentle kiss. His beard tickles my cheeks, but I fully participate in the kiss. He deepens the angle of his mouth and I feel the passion all the way to my toes. The kiss is no longer gentle or tentative. It's as if Max wants to show me without words what he's feeling. I return his passion in full.

Knock! Knock!

Hailey slowly opens the door and peeks inside. I'm still in Max's embrace and he doesn't pull away. She giggles. "Sorry for the interruption, but the Fergusons are here for their appointment."

Max groans and looks at me. "Okay, give me five minutes."

Hailey smiles and disappears, closing the door behind her.

I smile up at Max. He smiles back at me. Being in his embrace after the past two horrible weeks is like getting a slice of chocolate cake on my birthday. My heart zings with joy. I see the joy echoed back in Max's eyes.

"Can we continue this later?" he says.

I nod.

"I have a meeting tonight, but I'm free tomorrow. How about dinner?"

I stand on my tippy toes and kiss him again, then whisper, "Yes, that sounds perfect." I rub his scruffy beard. "You need to trim this though."

Max chuckles. "Duly noted." He then takes my hand and walks me to the door. Before he opens it, he gives me one more gentle kiss. "I'll be counting the minutes until I see you again."

I blush like a teenager and leave the room, waving at Hailey as I exit the office. Happiness bubbles over inside me and I feel like I'm walking on sunshine. I now understand what the song is about.

Chapter Seventeen

Max

The meeting with the Fergusons dragged on and on. Hailey finally saved me from purgatory when she pretended I had an urgent phone call. It's going to be a challenge working with this couple because they want to discuss every decision ad nauseum, down to what type of finishing nails we use in the baseboards. Seriously?

I admit, I was a little distracted during their meeting after Maddie poured out her soul to me. Her story broke my heart while at the same time mending it. Rather than trying to understand her point of view, I'd let my anger dictate how I reacted when I saw her with the other guy. In some ways she's like an innocent virgin even though she's been married. I respect and cherish that and will treat her with kid gloves. I love her so much it almost hurts.

Hailey was as excited about my making up with Maddie as I was. I'm sure she's told the entire family by now. Quinn texted me a few minutes ago: "Way to go Bro!" It's just a matter of time before I hear from Ash and Mom.

I'd be on my way to see Maddie tonight except I have my first mentoring session with my new mentee, Jamal. He expressed during one of our phone conversations that he loves pizza, so I'm meeting him at Joe's Pizza Barn. His grandmother is going to drop him off and then come back and get him. Jamal's background information indicated that his grandmother raised him until a few months ago.

When I walk in, the restaurant is already crowded with families and young couples sitting at the round café tables scattered around the room. I chuckle when I see teenage lovebirds holding hands or sharing a slice of pizza. They make me feel old, but I can't wait to bring Maddie here.

I recognize Jamal from his photo in the information I was given. He's sitting at the long bench across the front of the waiting area reading a book. His legs barely touch the floor, and the ugly green sweatshirt and faded blue jeans he's wearing hang on his skinny frame. His tight, curly black hair looks like he's trying to grow it into an afro, and it springs up in curly tufts all over his head.

"Jamal?" I stand directly in front of him and speak before he looks up.

His head raises and a smile splits his face. "Are you Mr. Connor?" he says, putting his book back in his backpack.

I nod. "Call me Max." We shake hands and his small hand is engulfed by my big one. I'm struck by the fact that he acts so polite and mature beyond his years.

"Is a booth okay?" I ask since he's the only one in the waiting area and a booth just opened. He trails behind me as I stride over to grab the spot. When I look back, Jamal is walking slowly, uneven hips making the process look both painful and difficult. He swings one leg forward, then swivels his hips and swings the other leg forward. Next time I'll know to slow my pace. His information mentioned he had a leg injury when he was two years old. But I didn't know it impacted his ability to walk.

Jamal's wide smile indicates that his awkward walking motion no longer bothers him. He plops down on his side of the booth, the red fake leather squeaking as he awkwardly adjusts his position. He then picks up a menu, reading it with great concentration.

"What kind of pizza do you like?" I say while also scanning the menu.

"Pepperoni!" He grins back at me.

I raise an eyebrow. "No other toppings? Just pepperoni?"

He looks like the answer should be self-evident. "I'm not a big fan of vegetables, Mr. Connor."

I laugh, a big belly laugh at both the expression on his face and his comment about vegetables. Yep. He's a typical eight-year-old.

The waitress stops by with waters. I order the pizza and a beer for me. Jamal orders a Sunkist soda. He informs the waitress that the orange juice in the soda is a healthy choice. She looks at me as we both suppress a laugh.

"What were you reading while you were waiting?" I nod towards his backpack.

He beams at the question and sits up straighter in the booth. "A book about baseball stats and how they use them for an advantage during games. It's called *Moneyball.*"

My eyes widen and I almost choke on my beer at the fact that an eight-year-old is reading a book like that.

"That's impressive! Do you like sports and statistics?"

The words are barely out of my mouth before Jamal's answering with a passion beyond his years. "I love sports! The intellectual side of the game really interests me, especially with . . ." His gaze moves down to his legs. "With my, you know, limited motion."

I nod and he barrels on.

"Grams and Mom always tell me that I can enjoy the strategy side of sports just as much as playing them myself. So, I learn as much as I can about all sports and the numbers that go with them." He pauses for a quick breath. "For instance, baseball has all sorts of pitching numbers like earned run average, strike outs, and stuff. But football is all about passing and rushing yards. So, all sports are different and interesting! I just started reading another book about golf. You might find it interesting . . ." He rummages around in his backpack and pulls out *Ben Hogan's Five Lessons: The Modern Fundamentals of Golf,* handing it across the table to me.

I open the front cover of the well-worn book and see the Connor's Grove library sticker on the first page. "You've read all of this?"

"Naw, not yet. I'm on page twenty-one but it's very enlightening. Next time I watch the PGA on TV, I'm gonna see how many of Mr. Hogan's five lessons they employ."

I squint over at him and tease. "Are you sure you're only eight?"

He giggles in his high-pitched child's voice. "Mom says the same thing."

Leaning back in the booth I wonder what I can mentor the kid in. He's well behaved, interesting, and knowledgeable. Maybe he can teach me a few things.

The steaming hot pizza arrives, and we dig in. Jamal eats several pieces, which makes me doubt whether he had any lunch.

"So, Jamal, what would you like mentoring in? Do you need help with some of your subjects in school?"

He chews on the bite he just took before he answers. This kid has good manners. "I'm terrible at math. Grams says that math will be a big help in understanding all the sports numbers, but it just makes my head hurt."

I laugh. "I know a professor who teaches mathematics. I'm sure I can ask her to help you."

"A girl who knows math?" He looks skeptical.

Okay, we need to work on his appreciation for the opposite sex. I grin. "Yes, she's a very nice lady. I'll introduce you to her."

He wiggles in his seat. "Mr. Connor—ahh, Max—there is one more thing."

I nod, happy that he has a list. "What is it?"

He hesitates. I wait patiently for his reply.

"I'd love to go to a professional baseball or football game. The Twins and the Vikings are my favorites! Mom says we don't have the budget to fill those snobby athletes' pockets with gold. But I just wanna go to a game. You know what I mean?"

I try to hide my smile at his mom's words. I wonder what's behind that statement but don't probe any further. "Jamal, I would be honored to take you to a baseball *and* a football game! We'll talk to your grandmother when she picks you up to make sure she agrees and decide on a date to go see the Twins."

He grins from ear to ear and eats another piece of the gooey pizza. I'll have the waitress box up what's left and send it home with him.

On my way home I can't get rid of the silly grin on my face. I didn't know how much I would enjoy this mentoring thing. Being with Jamal also made me realize how much I like kids. I'm going to have to persuade Maddie into having at least two. My grin gets wider.

Chapter Eighteen

Maddie

You'd think I was getting ready for my first date ever with all the time and money I've spent! My wonderful sister-in-law and BFF is helping me pick out a new dress. Without her assistance, I would be lost. I want to look extra nice for my first official date with Max, and since Jack died, I haven't had a special occasion that warranted new clothes.

"Maddie, come look at this one! You'll look fabulous in this."

Becca just had her baby, a little girl named Ella Jackie. Tears filled my eyes when she told me the Jackie is named after Jack. Since she's still sporting fifteen extra pounds of baby weight, Becca is living vicariously through me right now. If she wasn't along, I would spend half the time and half the money on this outfit. But you only live once!

I look at the creation she's holding up. Frowning, I say, "Isn't it a little too low cut? My, um, girls will be hanging out in that."

She emits a scoffing sound. "Don't you want the sexy man to gulp when he sees you?"

I hold up my hand. "Okay, I'll try it on."

Becca pushes me towards the dressing room. She paces outside the door while I undress. "I keep leaking milk! Is it noticeable?" She flings open the door when I have the dress only halfway over my head. I pull the dress down quickly to hide my underwear, and she smiles at the result. "Look at you!" She claps her hands, turning me towards the mirror.

The misty green fabric drapes elegantly over my body, highlighting every contour to its best. The V-neck is low cut, but you see just a hint of cleavage, while the material clings to my chest making it look like I have D-cups rather than B-cups. The skirt hits me mid-thigh, showing off more leg than I'm used to. I turn back and forth in the dress, watching it swirl seductively around me.

I bite my lip, knowing the dress looks sexy and alluring on me. "It might be too flamboyant. Not my usual style," pops out of my mouth.

Becca rolls her eyes while dabbing at the front of her shirt with a napkin. Two round moist spots draw attention to her obviously leaking mammary glands. Her harried appearance tells me that juggling a "terrible twos" toddler and a newborn is taking its toll on my otherwise organized sister-in-law. "Nonsense! You look gorgeous. Max won't be able to keep his hands off you."

I shake my head. "We're going out to dinner. At a public place."

She laughs. "Afterwards, silly, when he brings you home."

My pulse rate escalates at those words. I hadn't thought much about that portion of the evening.

Becca pats my back. "Just breathe Maddie. This date will end much better than the one with that professor!"

Blushing, the corners of my mouth quirk up. Now that I've repaired my relationship with Max I can almost smile about the disastrous date with Professor Bolton.

Once I'm back in my street clothes, Becca tugs me to the shoe department where she finds a pair of black high heels that make my legs look even longer. "What a find! Come-hither shoes and a dress. The man is going to have a heart attack when he sees you."

I glance around the store in case anyone else hears her words. "Shh! I'll be too embarrassed to wear this if you keep going on and on about Max's reaction."

She giggles. "Trust me. His tongue is gonna hang out of his mouth."

I roll my eyes and walk to the register to pay.

~*~

When Max arrives, my nerves are already shot worrying about his reaction to this dress and heels. I almost changed five times before he got here, into something more conservative. But I kept hearing Becca saying, *Come on Maddie, the man oozes sex appeal. Show him how sexy a professor can be!*

I take a deep breath and open the door. Max is standing on the front porch looking like a million bucks. Sexy doesn't even come close to describing him. His dark gray suit fits his body perfectly, showing off those broad shoulders. The ice-blue tie matches his eyes. I'm going to keel over before we even leave the house.

A slow smile spreads across this face. He takes my hand, kissing the palm while never taking his eyes off me. "Madeleine, you look more beautiful than words can describe." This time he says my formal name with reverence and adoration. *Swoon!* Tingles run up my arm.

Fibi breaks the intimate haze when he barks at Max's feet. My date bends down, rubbing the black and white dog. "Hey boy, you look pretty good yourself." Fibi barks twice as if in agreement. Max winks up at me as he continues to pet my sweet border collie.

He stands after showering a few more minutes of love on Fibi. I laugh internally as I remember that William wouldn't even touch my dog.

Realizing that I haven't said anything since Max arrived, I quickly try to fill the void. "Do you want to come sit down, or should we be going?" I motion towards the living room sofa.

Max looks at the watch on his wrist. "We'd better get going. The reservation is at 6:30 and we have to drive to Stillwater."

He helps me into my lightweight coat. When we get to his massive pickup, he picks me up like I weigh nothing and tucks me safely into the seat. When he joins me in the truck, I lean over and kiss him lightly on the cheek.

"The beard looks much better," I whisper in his ear.

He turns, taking me by surprise, and kisses me deeply. Several seconds and a few satisfied sounds from me later, he pulls back. "We better get going or we aren't going to get out of the driveway."

I laugh.

~*~

The restaurant in Stillwater is a charming restored Victorian home with a romantic vibe. I've heard all sorts of positive reviews about the place and can't wait to try it. Obviously, this isn't a place you go to with a girlfriend.

Since it's a Thursday night the restaurant isn't crowded. A waiter wearing black pants, a crisp white shirt, and a red bow tie seats us, handing us each a giant menu. I guess they felt compelled to list everything on one page, or maybe the printing costs were cheaper for this format.

After I spend several minutes being overwhelmed by the vast menu, Max breaks the silence. "Decide what you want?" He smiles at me with that cheeky grin, making my heart turn summersaults in my chest.

I take a calming breath. "They certainly have a wide selection," I reply as I try to suppress a giggle.

Max laughs. "You got that right. Maybe we should stick to the special."

I nod. The special that the waiter mentioned when he seated us did sound good. I haven't had rainbow trout in forever.

Our waiter returns, hovering at the side of the table. He turns his gaze to me. "What would the lady like?"

"I'll have the special."

He nods, scribbling on a small notebook. "Baked potato okay?"

"Yes. Please put the butter and sour cream on the side."

Max chimes in before the waiter even looks over at him. "I'll have the same but make mine a loaded baked potato."

I raise an eyebrow and grin. He shrugs.

Once the waiter disappears, Max reaches across the table and takes my hand. "Maddie, I've been looking forward to this all week. You look gorgeous in that dress."

My face heats as I blush at his comment. "You realize that it's only been a day since you saw me, right?" I tease.

He rolls his eyes. "Well, it felt like a whole week."

We both laugh.

A bread basket overflowing with different kinds of bread is deposited in the middle of the table by a twenty-something with a nose ring and black eyeshadow. She has a goth look that's a little scary, but her shy smile is friendly as she refills our water glasses.

After the interruption, Max passes the bread and we both enjoy the carbohydrate goodness. The thin slices of rye bread slathered in butter hit the spot.

"So, what did you do yesterday? You said you had a meeting after work?" I've been curious about that since Max mentioned it.

He smiles. "I'm mentoring an eight-year-old as part of the Big Brother program we just kicked off in Connor's Grove. My brother Jacob launched the thing a few weeks ago."

"I wanted to go to the kickoff, but the math department had a mixer with new students so I couldn't attend."

He nods. "You can help me with my mentee. He needs some tutoring in math."

My heart does a happy flip. Anytime I can help a young person understand math, I'm in. "I'd be happy to tutor him. Tell me more about his background."

A fond smile crosses Max's face. He's already attached to his mentee, I can tell.

"His name is Jamal. He's the nicest, most well-behaved eight-year-old boy I've ever met. He was injured when he was two and isn't able to walk very well, but it doesn't seem to bother him. Yesterday I met him at Joe's Pizza Barn and boy, can he pack away the pizza! Although he wouldn't try anything other than pepperoni."

I nod, remembering my cousin Keith at that age. He wouldn't let a vegetable get within ten feet of him.

"It's not clear what happened to his dad. His grandmother enrolled him in the Big Brother program so Jamal would have a positive male influence in his life. The kid eats and breathes sports but has never been to a professional sporting event before. We're going to a Twins game in two weeks, and I'd love for you to come with us."

Without needing to take even a second to consider Max's surprise invitation, I reply, "That sounds great! I haven't gone to a Twins game in a while. Plus, I'll be attending with two fabulous guys. How could a girl turn that down?"

Max chuckles as the waiter arrives with our meals. We dig into the delicious food, exchanging small talk and enjoying the gourmet taste sensations. No wonder this restaurant is getting rave reviews.

~*~

As we approach my house, my palms start to sweat, and my heart rate accelerates. The sexy guy next to me doesn't seem to notice. What will he expect when we get home? What do I expect to happen? What do I want to happen?

Questions cloud my brain and churn my stomach. Thoughts of intimacy give me heart palpitations. Am I ready to take our relationship to that level? Will I disappoint Max? As usual, I overthink and overanalyze everything.

Flashing lights catch my attention as soon as we turn the corner. They appear to be coming from the Robinson's house next door.

"Looks like your neighbor has an emergency with all those flashing lights," Max says as he slows, turning carefully into my driveway.

A paramedic vehicle along with a firetruck are parked at the curb beside Gloria's house. My eyebrows draw together as worry clutches my heart. "The Robinsons are getting up in age. I hope nothing terrible has happened!"

"Charlie and Gloria Robinson are your neighbors?" Max asks.

I turn to look at him. "Yes, why?"

He nods. "I forgot where they live. Their son Doug is best friends with my brother Quinn, and the three of us used to hang out in high school. The house used to be painted yellow, so I didn't recognize it."

Anxiety laces my words. "Gloria and Charlie have been so supportive since Jack . . ." My voice trails off. I promised myself I wouldn't mention my husband tonight yet here I am talking about him again. I clear my throat. "They're like second parents to me. I better go see what's going on."

Max pulls me closer. "But first, I have to do this," he says in his gravelly voice and then proceeds to make me breathless with a kiss. His lips encourage me to participate and I do so with a zeal I thought I would never feel again. After several beats we pull apart.

"I'll go with you to check on the Robinsons," he says, gazing in my eyes for several seconds after that mind-numbing kiss. His big hands cup my face and he looks as affected as I am by the chemistry we obviously share.

Max gets out and helps me down from the large vehicle. Taking my hand, we walk over to my neighbors. Relief and disappointment fight to take over my emotions. I have a reprieve from worrying about whether I want to take my relationship with Max to a more physical level. The safe, careful Maddie is happy about that outcome. But the passionate Maddie wishes she could experience more of Max's kisses.

Chapter Nineteen

Max

Charlie Robinson's heart attack turned out to be indigestion from spicy tacos. The paramedics insisted he go to the hospital for tests, so Maddie went along with Gloria, who was having a nervous breakdown over the situation. I fully supported Maddie's desire to help her neighbor but was disappointed at how our evening ended.

I probably need to take it slow with Maddie. During the drive back from the restaurant she became more and more quiet, as if she was suddenly nervous in my presence. I assume if Jack is the only man she ever dated, he was also the only man she's ever been intimate with. I'm happy to give her all the time she needs, with many kisses sprinkled in to urge her along. I grin at the prospect.

My phone dings and dances across my desk with an incoming text.

Maddie: Fibi and I have an Agility competition on Saturday. Do you want to come with us?

An invitation to spend time with my favorite human—and favorite dog.

Max: Count me in! What time should I pick you up?

Maddie: The competition is down in Rochester, so we need a couple hours to get down there and set up. How about 7 am?

Max: Sounds good. I can't wait to see you (heart Emoji)

Maddie: (Smiley face Emoji)

~*~

My companions are ready and waiting when I arrive. Maddie has her Agility equipment sitting in the driveway. Her tight blue jeans and red V-neck shirt hug all her curves perfectly, as confirmed by my roving eyes. She greets me at the door, and I pull her in for what I thought would be a quick kiss. Instead, the chemistry between us flares up like a fast-moving brush fire. In seconds my heart is racing and I'm out of breath. She tightens her arms around my neck as we thoroughly explore each other's lips. After several seconds, our mouths reluctantly pull apart.

The black and white dog sits at our feet, looking up at us and patiently waiting for our attention to be directed at him. I glance down and that's all the encouragement he needs. Fibi jumps up, tail wagging furiously as he circles around us. I feel Maddie laughing since she's still wrapped firmly in my arms.

She whispers in my ear, "I think he's jealous. He's used to being king of the house."

I lean my forehead against hers and sigh. "It's probably lucky he broke up our kissing session. I was rapidly losing track of time. Woman, I can't resist you."

Maddie rubs her hand on my cheek, smiling into my eyes. "I can say the same, Mr. Connor." Her face turns an adorable shade of pink.

Bark! Bark!

"Fibi's done waiting." I nod towards him as Maddie slowly pulls out of my arms.

She bends down, gently stroking the beautiful creature. Looking back up at me, she says, "Let's get going. I can't wait for you to see Fibi compete. He's going to win a ribbon today!"

Bark! Bark!

Apparently Fibi agrees.

~*~

Maddie loads her cooler, human snacks, extra Agility equipment, dog bowl, and dog treats in the extended cab while Fibi plops on the floor behind my seat. Luckily I have this roomy truck for all the stuff she's bringing. At least my date is well prepared.

After a few miles, I break the silence currently being drowned out by a Blake Shelton song. "Maddie, I can't believe I've never asked you this, but where did you grow up? What did your dad do?"

"My dad was a Professor at the University of Minnesota. We lived in the Falcon Heights neighborhood of Saint Paul for many years." She has a faraway look on her face, as if she's remembering the old neighborhood.

I grin. "Let me guess, your dad was a math professor."

"Nice try, Connor, but my dad was a Physics professor. My mom was the math professor."

My eyes widen and I shake my head. No wonder she's a brainiac with parents like that. "That's some high IQ pedigree, Professor! Do your parents still live in Saint Paul?"

A sad expression crosses Maddie's face. "No, they were much older when they had me. Dad passed five years ago and Mom three years ago."

I reach over and squeeze her hand. "I'm sorry to hear that."

She nods.

"What made you and Jack choose Connor's Grove?" Now I'm the one mentioning her dead husband. I cringe as my foot keeps inserting itself into my mouth.

My companion doesn't seem to notice my slip. "Jack's family all lived here. You know Jim and Rebecca, but his parents also used to live here. They retired and moved to Florida about four years ago. Jack's mom wanted to be closer to her sister, Gretta Peterson." She pauses and looks over at me. "The Petersons own that campground on Highway 12."

I glance over at Maddie. "Ah, the famous Minnehaha Campground."

The corner of her mouth quirks up. "You know it? Have you camped there?"

Keeping my eyes on the deserted road in case we come across a tractor or other farm equipment, I nod. "Hailey lived there for three months when she first moved to town."

Gasping, Maddie spurts out, "Lived there?"

"She was strapped financially and couldn't afford any other place. From what I hear, the Petersons practically adopted her."

Out of the corner of my eye I see Maddie nodding. "Ah, that explains the gnome collection."

A belly laugh erupts from deep inside me. Fibi sticks his head between the seats to see what's so funny. "So you've seen Hailey's collection?"

"Yep. I had coffee with her after our yoga class last week and she proudly showed me all her figurines. She mentioned her collection is nowhere near as large as Gretta's extensive collection." Maddie sniggers. "Did you know that Gretta heads up the national gnome fan club or something like that?"

I chuckle. "Does every woman in Connor's Grove collect those things? My mom even has a collection."

My beautiful companion rolls her eyes. "Nope. Not me. Did you see any gnomes in my house?"

I squeeze her arm. "Maybe they're hidden in a back bedroom. Maybe you're a closet gnome collector?"

We both laugh. I focus back on the highway, slowing down as we enter a small burg with ten dilapidated homes and a grain elevator. A wide spot in the road, as Mom calls them.

"So, Max, are you related to the Connors who Connor's Grove is named after?"

Pushing out my chest and sitting up straighter, I say proudly, "Yes, my great-grandparents founded the town. They lived near a grove of elm trees and people would give directions by saying 'the grove near the Connors.' Once the town sprang up, the name evolved into Connor's Grove."

My companion smacks me on my arm and grins. "Wow, town royalty! Do I need to curtsy in your presence?"

"Why yes, Professor, please do!"

Miles pass as we swap stories about other quirky characters we both know in Connor's Grove. Maddie shares the fact that she's taught nineteen different Vandervoldts, all of which are either siblings or cousins. The Vandervoldts are second only to the Connors in prestige and influence in our small town.

"Max, do you ever think that the saying is true—it's a small world? Look at all the people who are interconnected in Connor's Grove."

I contemplate her statement for a few seconds. "Yeah, like six degrees of Kevin Bacon, but it's six degrees of the Vandervoldts or Petersons!"

She laughs. "Exactly!"

Bark! Bark! Fibi draws our attention as we enter the outskirts of Rochester. He perks up and stares out the passenger window as if he recognizes that we're near our destination.

"We've competed here a couple of times. Fibi knows the town," Maddie explains with a shrug.

I smile. *Genius dog. Genius owner.*

Chapter Twenty

Maddie

Holding the blue second-place ribbon, I smile for the camera while Fibi sits at attention at my feet. Max stands off to the side, grinning ear-to-ear like a proud parent.

"Thanks Maddie, we got all the photos we need. Good to see you and Fibi competing again," Joshua Hanson says as he smiles and shakes my hand. He's been a fixture in charge of Agility competitions throughout the state for many years.

"We were a little rusty, but it feels good to be back," I say to Joshua as he departs to interview the winning dog and owner.

Max walks over, pulling me into a bear hug and lifting me off my feet. "I'm so proud of you!" he says as I bask in the embrace. "Fibi and you are terrific! Only one-tenth of a second between you and the winning dog," he says as he shakes his head. "I'd call that a tie."

I tingle from head to foot while my heart does a triple summersault. Just a mere touch by hunky Mr. Connor and I want to melt at his feet. We gaze at each other while the crowd disperses around us.

Bark! Bark!

I laugh at Fibi's reminder that the event is over and it's time to pack everything up and leave. "We better get going! I packed sandwiches so we can eat in the truck before the long drive home."

Max chuckles. "Frugal and smart."

I blush at his teasing.

~*~

"Wake up, sleepyhead." Max's rumbly voice penetrates my consciousness. The gentle shaking of my shoulder brings me fully awake.

My eyes blink open, staring into an incredible pair of blue eyes. The sexy guy smiling at me makes my heart turn a flip-flop in my chest.

I glance out the window and see we're parked in front of my house. "I slept the whole way home!" Embarrassment floods my cheeks. He must think I'm the worst date ever.

His lips twitch. "Looks like the competition tired out both contestants." He nods towards Fibi, who's napping soundly behind my seat.

Putting my hand to my lips I suppress a smile. "We're both a little out of practice."

"And yet, you took second place. I'd say you both are incredible." He extends his hand, helping me down from the truck.

Fibi sits up, jumps to the front seat where I was just sitting, and hops to the ground. He runs around us, then sits patiently at the front door. Swiveling his head to look back at his human companions, he looks like if he could talk, he would say, "Get a move on!"

Yawning, I point to all my stuff packed behind the back seat. "Should we unload first?"

Max takes my hand, pulling me towards the door. "You and Fibi go inside and relax. I'll unpack the truck."

Once inside, I plop on the couch and watch Max unload. All those glorious muscles flexing under his tight shirt. I should feel guilty about being such a lazy observer, but I don't.

After several minutes I'm wide awake and Max has the truck unpacked.

"Can I make some coffee? I have some fresh baked zucchini bread. My garden is finally producing, and I have zucchini running out my ears . . ." I realize I'm rambling, so I snap my mouth shut in case I mention the abundance of tomatoes and green peppers as well.

Chuckling, Max comes over and sits beside me. He pushes a stray hair behind my ear. "I'd love a cup of coffee, but are you too tired for my company?"

I grab his hand, pulling him up from the couch with me. "Never! Come talk to me while I make the coffee." We walk hand in hand to the kitchen. Fibi is in his bed in the corner. He raises his head when we enter, then relaxes back down.

While I'm busy putting grounds into the coffee pot, Max takes a seat at the island. Knowing that he's watching me unnerves me, making me spill some of the grounds on the counter. I take a calming breath then count to ten, but Max's rumbly voice breaks my concentration. "I had a great time today. I'd never paid any attention to dog agility competitions. It's quite a fascinating sport, especially when one of the competitors is wearing tight blue jeans."

Turning, I look him straight in the eye. "Are you flirting with me Mr. Connor?"

He stands, walking slowly towards me. My heart rate escalates with each step he takes. His arms go around me, pulling me close to his well-defined chest. I swear I'd melt at his feet if he wasn't holding me upright.

"Is it working?"

For a second or two, I lose track of the conversation. My brain stalls at his question while I focus on all the maleness surrounding me.

He raises an eyebrow. Oh yeah, he asked if his flirting is working. Isn't it obvious? I'm acting like a flustered teenager on her first date.

"Yes, it's working," I reply in a breathless voice.

He leans in, taking my lips in a slow kiss. Our lips meld together as if they're meant to do this forever. I can't think, being pressed against him like this, I can only feel. Max is the center of my universe, enclosing me completely and I can't get enough of him. The feeling of his hard strength against my soft curves. My heart beating erratically in my chest. His lips encouraging mine to explore deeper, which I do.

Eventually Max pulls back, searching my eyes. "Right now, it feels like I won the blue ribbon."

My head drops back to his chest, hiding my blush. I gather myself together and find the bravery to tell him what's foremost on my mind—other than my all-consuming attraction to him.

I bite my lip, looking back up. "I'm not ready to . . ." *Say it Maddie!* I admonish myself for my cowardice. Clearing my throat, I try again, "I'm not ready to sleep with you Max. I'm sorry."

His arms still encircle me. He shakes his head. "Maddie, do you think that's the only thing I want from you?" The disappointment in his voice is evident.

"No, but we're moving quickly in that direction and it scares me." I rub his cheek and the stubble tickles my fingers. "What if I disappoint you? I'm just a nerdy math whiz."

I feel him chuckle against me. "Sweetheart, I don't want to rush you. I've waited five years for you. It's up to you to tell me when you're ready. Let's just enjoy each other's company. No pressure."

Relief spreads through my body. On my tippy toes, I place another kiss on his lips. He lets me set the pace and intensity. We kiss until I recognize that we need to stop. When I pull back, we both take deep, calming breaths.

"Do you still want that cup of coffee?"

He smiles. "Yes, and the zucchini bread."

Grinning, I turn back to the forgotten coffee pot to finish my task. Max takes a seat back at the island.

That's when it hits me square in my heart—I'm starting to fall in love with this guy.

Chapter Twenty-One

Max

"Max, when does the family get to meet your new girlfriend? How about you bring Maddie to Sunday's family meal? Everyone will be there." Mom is about as subtle as a wrecking ball. If I don't capitulate, she'll keep bringing this up all week. The phone calls will get more frequent and the arm twisting more forceful.

I mentally roll my eyes and sigh. "I'll check with her to see what her plans are on Sunday." Not exactly a firm commitment, but Mom will take it as one.

A loud squeal comes from the other end of the line. I hold the phone several inches away from my ear in case there's further exuberance from my overly enthusiastic parent. "Excellent! We eat at 12:30. See you then!"

Mom ends the call quickly in case I change my mind. I might as well get this over and issue the invitation to Maddie.

Max: Mom invited you to our family meal on Sunday. I'll never hear the end of it if I don't bring you!

I hold my breath waiting for her reply.

Maddie: Sounds fun! What time?

Whew! She doesn't know what she just agreed to, but I won't enlighten her.

Max: I'll pick you up at 12:15. We eat at 12:30.

Maddie: What can I bring?

Max: Yourself, a big appetite, and a thick skin (thumbs up Emoji)

Maddie: (laughing Emoji)

Is Maddie ready to meet the family?

~*~

My palms start sweating when I arrive to pick Maddie up. Hopefully the family doesn't scare her off.

She greets me at the door wearing black jeans and a fancy red blouse.

"You look gorgeous, as always." I pull her in for a quick kiss but, as usual, the chemistry between us roars to life. We kiss for what could be seconds or minutes. I lose track of time, focusing on the sexy woman in my arms.

A ringtone echoes loudly around the room, coming from Maddie's cell phone perched on the end table beside the sofa.

She wiggles away and giggles.

"Who's that? Friend checking up on your hot date?"

A red blush creeps across her cheeks as she walks over to quiet the noisy device. "I set a five-minute timer so we didn't lose track of time." She raises an eyebrow as if daring me to complain.

I smirk. "I do have a tendency to lose myself in the moment when I kiss you."

Maddie laughs and hits me in the arm. "That's an understatement, Connor!" She collects her things, including a plate of mouth-watering looking brownies. "I'm ready. Let's go!"

As we walk to my truck, I nod towards the plate in her hand. "You know you didn't have to bring anything."

"Are you kidding? Every Minnesota girl knows to bring something to a family dinner! That's protocol."

I roll my eyes, knowing Mom would say the same thing. "Okay, whatever you say Professor." But inside I'm smiling, thinking she'll fit in with my family perfectly.

~*~

My date smiles as the Connor clan gathers around her, barely letting her get in the door. We're holding hands, so I squeeze hers as the noisy throng surrounds us. She squeezes back.

Hailey comes over immediately, pulling Maddie into a firm hug. She whispers something in Maddie's ear that makes them giggle. They're probably commiserating about being the two outsiders in the bunch.

My big brother greets her next, shaking her hand. "Nice to meet you Maddie."

She nods. "Likewise."

The rest of the family follows suit as Jacob, Ash, Dad, and Gramps all give her handshakes or pats on the back. Ashleigh winks at me after her exchange with Maddie. *What did she tell her?*

"We're in the kitchen! Bring Maddie back so we can meet her," Mom bellows.

I tug Maddie from the crowd of Connors, propelling her along towards the kitchen.

"Be ready for an inquisition," I whisper in her ear.

As usual, Mom and Nana are bustling around the kitchen with last-minute food preparations. Ash and Hailey join us while the men hang back in the living room. *Smart guys.*

Mom comes around the island, waiting for an introduction. She usually isn't reticent about greeting someone new, so I'm a little befuddled. But then I remember Mom's awe at Maddie being a math professor, so I quickly make introductions.

"Mom, this is Maddie Henderson." I turn towards Maddie. "Maddie, this is my mom, Jeannie."

The two women hug like long lost friends, then Maddie offers the plate of brownies.

"Oh my! These look delicious, Maddie! You didn't have to bring anything!"

I give Maddie a "see I told you so look" but she ignores me.

"They're Gloria Robinson's recipe. She won a purple ribbon at the county fair for them, or so she tells me."

Nana smiles and waves from her position stirring something in a pot on the stove. "I'm Catherine, but you can call me Nana. Gloria is such a wonderful cook! I can't wait to try one."

Mom nods in agreement while setting the plate on the island, then returns to dishing up the roast, potatoes, and carrots onto a huge serving platter. I asked Mom to make something other than lasagna and explained why so we didn't create an awkward moment on Maddie's first visit.

In an instant, things turn chaotic as Mom assigns tasks like a drill sergeant. We all pitch in to carry the food, condiments, and drinks to the big dining room adjacent to the kitchen. The huge oblong oak table sports a festive tablecloth and is set with Mom's Sunday china and authentic silver flatware.

Once everyone is seated, Maddie leans in and whispers, "The food smells divine!"

"Hold hands everyone!" Mom interrupts the chit-chat going on around the table. Her overly loud voice is easily heard above the fray. All the Connors know the drill, so we quickly clasp the hand of the person on either side of us. I smile at Maddie sitting to my left as I take her hand in mine.

"Lord, thank you for the food and all the hands that helped prepare it. Keep our neighbors and family safe throughout the upcoming days. We are thankful for our new guest and hope that she shares many more meals with us. Amen."

Very subtle Mom.

I wink at Maddie and she smiles. *Amens* resound around the table.

We pass the overflowing serving dishes, then everyone digs in. Silverware clinks as hungry family members eat while exchanging brief small talk. Ash has another friendly altercation with Jacob about his lack of enthusiasm for her kale and spinach salad. He grudgingly puts a small tablespoon on his plate and then smirks at her. My sister and brother participate in this ritual every meal. Maddie chuckles beside me while the rest of the family ignores their drama.

"Jeannie, the roast beef is delicious. I love how tender it is," Maddie says after taking several bites.

Nana chimes in, "The key to a tender roast is . . ."

"Searing!" all the Connor men exclaim, exchanging high-fives. Hailey, Mom, and Maddie laugh while Ash glares at everyone.

Once the family settles down again, Maddie leans towards me. "What's the inside joke about the pot roast?"

I grin. "Ash tried to make it one time and it was tough as leather. Nana gave her a personal cooking class about how to sear the meat properly. My sister complained about all the attention paid to her failure at cooking pot roast. So it's become a family joke."

We feast while my siblings ask my guest random questions which they probably conspired on before the meal. Things like: how long she's been teaching at the community college, what classes she likes best, and how many students she has this semester.

Leave it to Ash to ask the most embarrassing question of all. "Hey, Maddie, what was Max like as your student?"

Maddie's mouth twitches. "Well, he was smart and usually had the best score on exams." My chest puffs out, but then she continues . . . "He also had the most interesting defenses when he didn't get his homework done. That semester I swear he singlehandedly framed an entire house himself by the number of times that excuse came up."

Silence reigns for a few seconds because the table can't believe what my date revealed. When Ash cackles, that breaks the ice and everyone laughs except for me. I even see Mom wiping her eyes on her apron.

Maddie pats me on the back and mouths, "Sorry." But her expression tells me "not sorry."

Once my family settles down again, big brother Quinn takes a more serious tack, "What classes are you teaching during the summer semester?"

Maddie pauses and puts her fork back on her plate. "I'm teaching Calculus 101 and Differential Equations this time around."

Murmurs go around the table at the impressive response. I puff my chest out in pride at my brilliant date. Gramps adds, "What's Different Equations?"

The professor sweetly replies, "A differential equation is an equation with a function and one or more of its derivatives. We typically use them to represent the laws of nature such as heat flow—"

Groans around the table cut Maddie off. Nine pairs of eyes (including mine) stare at her with a mixture of awe and consternation.

Laughing she says, "TMI?"

"Yes!" The Connors reply, then everyone joins Maddie's laughter.

I lean over and give her a kiss on the cheek. She blushes.

Ash breaks the somewhat awkward moment by bringing out Maddie's plate of brownies from the kitchen. While Hailey and Ash clear the empty dinner plates, the brownie plate makes a circuit around the table. Quinn kindly takes one for his beloved, but no one looks out for Ashleigh. When she returns, there's only crumbs remaining.

"What! No one saved me a brownie?" she wails.

My sweetheart quickly passes her untouched brownie over to Ash. I split my brownie and hand the other half to the professor, who gives me a dazzling smile.

Dad, who's positioned at the head of the table, nods at me then says, "Max must really like this one if he's willing to share his dessert."

The table roars.

Chapter Twenty-Two

Maddie

"Go Twins!" the adorable kid next to me shouts, fist pumping in the air. Max and I exchange a humorous look over his curly head. It's rather obvious this is Jamal's first Twins game and he's determined to be an enthusiastic fan.

Max rises from his seat on the change of inning. "Does anyone want anything? I'm going to get another hot dog." We've already consumed five hot dogs, three biggie sodas, and a bag of caramel corn between the three of us.

"I want another hot dog! With lots of ketchup!" Jamal gestures wildly with his thin arms, making sure he gets Max's attention.

I point at the kid. "Where are you putting all this food?" Looking at his diminutive frame, you would never guess that he could eat this much.

Jamal giggles.

"Maddie, are you good?" My sweet boyfriend says.

Patting my full stomach, I nod and say, "I'm good."

Max squints at me. "How about a chocolate sundae in one of those helmet cups?"

"Oh! Oh! I'll have one of those, too!" Jamal practically jumps from his seat as he shouts out the order.

I snicker. "How about I split one with you?" I say to Max.

He laughs. "I knew you couldn't turn down chocolate!"

As he turns to leave, I try to hand him a ten-dollar bill, but he waves me off, then disappears.

The kid turns to me once Max is out of ear shot and says in the most matter-of-fact voice, "I think he had to pee but he didn't want you to know." He then guffaws as if he told a joke.

Surprised by the kid's frank statement, I snort and laugh loudly. Several heads in our row swivel, looking in my direction. I see them chuckling at Jamal's bathroom humor.

The diminutive fan looks proud of himself at my loud, embarrassing snort. He's a typical eight-year-old boy for sure.

As the Twins take the field, Jamal shares his baseball insights with me, which I don't need but kindly accept. "See how the third baseman is shifted so far towards second base? That means the next batter is a pull hitter," my companion explains.

I nod. "Is that so?"

Just as Max indicated, Jamal is smart beyond his years. He's a voracious reader who wants to impart all the knowledge he learns to anyone who will listen. Apparently, he read *Total Baseball* from cover-to-cover prior to today's game. He even brought the encyclopedic tome with him and has referred to it several times.

The crack of a bat draws our attention back to the field. One of the Twins' outfielders catches the flyball neatly in his glove. The crowd and, of course, Jamal cheer loudly.

Once the action settles down, I say, "Jamal, I want to set up some math tutoring sessions as soon as school starts again next month. We can keep on top of new concepts so you master them before exams."

What I assume is a kind offer is met with a nose wrinkle by Jamal. "Miss Maddie, can we talk about math later? I need to focus on the game right now."

I swallow my laughter at his polite yet firm response. "Sure. But you let me know as soon as you need help with math. Okay?"

His stares intently at the field and gives a small nod.

Max confided in me that Jamal is skeptical about a woman's knowledge in math. So I'll need to win him over.

Right after the Twins get the third out, Max returns carrying a tray loaded with food. He hands it to me, then retrieves napkins and three plastic spoons from his pocket.

The hot dogs smell yummy and my stomach growls in protest that I didn't order one. Max whispers in my ear, "I'll share my hot dog with you."

I grin, happy to oblige in helping consume the ballpark meat product. "I'll hold the sundae while you eat your dog," I say as eager fingers reach for some of the food. Jamal smiles with the hot dog in his hand and settles back in his seat.

Max unwraps the dog, feeding me bites and giving me sips of soda while I hold the two melting sundaes in my lap. The three of us snarf down the dogs, partly because they're delicious but also so we can move to the ice cream before it's just a puddle.

Max and I smile goofy smiles at each other, which our young companion notices.

"You guys keep giving each other goo-goo eyes. When are you getting married?"

Max's eyes widen. He pauses during the hot dog feeding fest long enough to give me a wink.

I wink back.

"I haven't even asked her yet, buddy."

Jamal giggles as if Max told a funny joke. His laughter is contagious, so Max and I join in.

The kid's innocent comment forces me to do some much-needed soul searching. Does my relationship with Max feel a little stalled? Marrying Max would be both terrifying and exhilarating, but he's never mentioned marriage to me. At some point I need to share my concerns with him about having children. Seeing Max with Jamal exemplifies the fact that he loves kids. What if I can't have any?

"I thought you were hungry?" Max teases, drawing me back from my musing.

He has ketchup on his mouth, so I let him know by pointing to the corner of my mouth. He leans over and kisses me smack on the lips, smearing the ketchup on my lips.

I glare at him while daintily wiping my mouth with a napkin, and he laughs.

A small hand snags one of the melting helmets. I hand him a spoon.

Holding the other melting treat, I give Max a spoon and we share the ice cream. I try to hog most of the chocolate sauce, but Max blocks my attempts with his spoon. The ice cream disappears in only a few seconds as we race to see who can spoon the fastest. Since a lot of the chocolate has settled to the bottom, I pull the container out of Max's reach and quickly lap up the sauce.

"You're a chocoholic Madeleine," my boyfriend growls in my ear.

I shrug and continue to lick the bowl clean. He kisses me again, getting another taste of the chocolate sauce.

"Delicious," he says with a smirk. *Does he mean the chocolate or me?*

Once the food is consumed, I put our waste inside the paper tray and stuff it under my seat. The 50,000 other fans at the ballpark are doing the same thing, so I don't feel even a tinge of guilt.

We relax and watch the game. During periods of action, we all watch intently. When there are lulls, Max and I chat while our companion refers to his baseball encyclopedia, offering tips and commentary. It's like having a mini game analyst with us.

In the sixth inning, the Twins load up the bases. The three of us sit forward in our seats, glued to the action. Everyone in the ballpark holds their breath when the Twins' best hitter strides to the plate.

Crack!

Center Fielder Byron Buxton hits a long ball towards where we're sitting. I watch the arc of the ball and realize it's coming right towards us. Hopping from my seat, I stretch my arm up, neatly catching the ball. It smacks my palm, but I hang on despite the sting. The crowd cheers at the home run while those in the vicinity next to us cheer for my catch. I quickly sit back down, not wanting to draw further attention to myself.

"Here, Jamal, a souvenir from the game," I say as I hand him the ball.

Both my companions stare at me, openmouthed.

Max breaks the silence. "That was a heck of a catch! And barehanded nonetheless."

Jamal chimes in, "Miss Maddie how did you know how to catch that?"

I chuckle. "I played softball in high school. I was an outfielder."

A guy seated behind us says, "Nice catch lady!"

Another guy adds, "You'll be on the ESPN highlight reel for sure!"

Cowering lower in my seat, I blush at the praise.

Several minutes pass and two men wearing official-looking stadium uniforms stop at the end of our row. They point to me then walk past several people to approach our seats.

What do they want? Surely fans can still catch baseballs if they don't interfere with play.

"Ma'am, are you the person who caught the ball?" The older guy asks in a polite voice.

"Yes," I reply as Jamal holds up the ball for him to see.

"Congratulations!" The younger guy chimes in. "That was the 10,000th ball caught by a fan in Target Field." He then hands me a

Twins jersey, Twins baseball cap, and two tickets to an upcoming game.

I stare in shock at the gifts and the milestone my catch attained.

"We'd like to get a picture with you and your family," the older guy says as he pulls a camera out of his pocket. I don't correct him about the family comment as Max, Jamal, and I lean close together with Jamal holding up the baseball and me clutching my winnings.

"We'll email you a copy if you give me your email address."

I scribble it down on a paper younger guy hands me, then the two men disappear.

"Wow!" Max says. Other people near us in the crowd nod in agreement.

I put the hat on Jamal's head but keep the jersey for myself. I'll give Max the tickets after the game.

"Miss Maddie, can you sign the ball for me?" Jamal holds up the ball. A guy behind us hands me a sharpie and I sign the ball with a flourish.

The kid looks happily at the ball in his hand, then up at me. "That's the best catch I've ever seen in my whole life!"

Everyone around us laughs at that announcement. I grin.

Chapter Twenty-Three

Max

Dating Maddie is like a dream come true. As I get to know her better, I'm falling more and more in love with her. I told her no pressure on taking our relationship to the next level and I meant it. But, what can I do to break down her barriers and win her heart completely? I'm not sure we're on the same page as to how quickly our relationship should move forward, and what forward really means. Does she want to get married again? Does she want to have kids?

Quinn strolls in while I'm squinting at the Fergusons' blueprints. They want yet another change to the layout. At this rate we won't get their house built until next year.

"Hey, Brother, what's up?" He doesn't usually stop by in the middle of the day.

"Thought you might be free for lunch. We don't have that many nice days left before the snow flies, so I needed to get out of the office." Quinn's observation is spot-on. This stint of Indian summer is going to end soon. In two weeks, September will be only a memory.

I roll up the blueprints. "Sure! Let's go to Joe's Pizza Barn. I have a craving for their gooey, greasy pizza."

My brother laughs.

We pass Hailey on the way out. She's been working overtime with all the invoices and orders. Connor Construction is running at full capacity.

"Sweetie, do you want to go to Joe's with us?" Quinn asks his wife.

She stands, planting a big kiss on his lips. Her stance as she hugs him is a little stiff—I wonder if the baby is big enough to get between them. She hasn't looked visibly pregnant yet, but surely that will come any day now. "Bring me two slices. Mr. Connor needs me to get all these invoices out today." She grins over at me. Quinn unconsciously rubs her belly then follows me out the door.

I can only hope that someday Maddie looks at me like that. Jamal's innocent question regarding marrying Maddie rattles around in my brain. Will she ever be ready to take that step?

~*~

Joe's is hopping even though it's past the rush hour. We snag a booth towards the back; place our usual order of pepperoni, sausage, and green peppers; then sip on the sodas our harried waitress bring us.

I break the ice. "Okay, what's up? The weather was a good excuse, but I know you have an ulterior motive."

Quinn's eye widen, then he smirks. "I'm on a data-gathering mission courtesy of Mom."

Of course! My relationship with Maddie isn't moving fast enough for Matchmaker Jeannie.

I play innocent. "Oh, what do you want to know?"

His lips twitch. "As you know, Mom's already planning a spring wedding for you and Maddie, but she's starting to worry at your slow pace. When are you going to ask the professor to marry you?"

I give my brother credit; he's laid all his cards on the table.

"The ball's in her court. I told her I wouldn't push and that she can let me know when she's ready to take our relationship to the next step."

My brother gives a skeptical eyebrow raise. "Do you think that's wise?"

He has a point. It's like one step forward and then two steps backward with Maddie. She needs to lead with her heart rather than that big brain of hers. Still, I frown back at him. "Let me remind you that you took your good old time in asking Hailey to marry you. In fact, if I remember correctly, it required Hailey getting hurt in a car accident to push you over the edge."

He blushes. "Desperate times called for desperate measures . . . But we're talking about you and the professor. You need a grand gesture—push her out of the comfort zone you're letting her languish in."

Big brother is correct. My relationship with Maddie has become a bit complacent and I can't seem to figure out how to move her forward without being pushy, without breaking my promise to give her time. She's not a risk-taker, so she just accepts this comfortable rapport we've settled into the last few months.

The waitress plops a steaming pizza on the table along with two plates. We're distracted for several minutes as we serve up the pizza and eat.

Quinn waves a slice at me. "What's a grand gesture that will get the ball moving again?" His words come out mumbled since he's chewing on pizza while he speaks.

"I don't know. A proposal on the Jumbotron at a Twins game?"

He nods as if considering the option I'd meant as a joke. "How about something a little less public?"

"I could show up with notecards at her front door and she can read them as I flash through them, declaring my love."

"Chicks love that movie! Hailey watches it all the time."

"How about I bring her a crumpled bag of Snappy Stop hamburgers?"

These are all clichéd ideas—the last one being done by Quinn himself.

"I think those have already been done," Captain Obvious replies with a smirk.

Well duh. "Okay, Big Brother, do you have any creative, unique ideas?"

He laughs. "No, but we can enlist Mom's help."

I hold up my hand. "No way! We are not enlisting Mom's or Nana's or Ash's help."

Picking up another slice, I take a big bite, chewing frantically and taking my frustration out on the pizza.

"Hey, she'll come around. Forget I said anything. Let's talk about whether the Vikings will be able to win the division."

Happy for the change of subject, I nod. "Cousins needs to pass to his wide receivers down field more often."

That sets Quinn off, and we argue for the rest of lunch as to the best game-winning strategy for the Vikes, while I wonder what's the best game-winning strategy for Maddie and me.

Chapter Twenty-Four

Maddie

Rebecca stares me down across her dining table. I feel like I've come full circle asking for relationship advice. Again. "Come on, Maddie. Spill it! You didn't come here just to load me up with your zucchini bread. Which, by the way, I'm grateful for."

Two coffee mugs and a plate of the aforementioned bread sit on the table between us. This does feel like déjà vu from months ago.

"I'm scared to let Jack go," I blurt it out, much like yanking a Band-Aid from a hairy leg. Painful for an instant and then it's over.

A line appears between her brows. "I thought you got over that. You're still dating Max, right?"

"Yes, I'm dating Max. We've been seeing each other three months now." I pause for several beats. "Becca, I keep dragging my feet in this relationship. I'm so confused!" I shake my head and my words come out as a high-pitched wail.

Her eyes widen. "What are you confused about?"

I bite my lower lip. "What if I let myself fall completely in love with Max and I forget Jack and all our happy memories? Am I just crushing after a gorgeous guy who makes my heart pound and my palms sweat? Do Max and I have a future?" The words spew from my mouth and I barely take a breath between sentences.

My sweet sister-in-law reaches across the table and takes my hand. "Let's address your concerns one by one . . ."

This feels like therapy. Maybe all I've been missing is someone to confide in and talk to about my doubts.

Becca smiles at me gently. "First, you have a big heart. I think there's plenty of space for both Max and Jack. You won't forget all your memories with your husband even though you'll be making new memories with Max."

A tear rolls down my cheek and plops on my hand. I motion with my chin for her to continue.

"Second, just because you and Max have great chemistry, it doesn't mean you don't love him. How would you feel if Max walked away from your relationship today?"

Her question confuses me. What's she getting at? "Well . . . I think I'd be crushed. He fills a void in my life that I didn't even realize I had until I met him . . ." I put my fingers over my lips as the truth hits me.

Becca beams. "That's love, Maddie." Her eyes twinkle. "You should know the answer to your last question—you have a future with Max because you love him."

I squeeze my eyes shut for a second because my next words are going to be the most difficult of all. "I may not be able to have children." My confession hangs in the air like an embarrassing body noise that everyone pretends didn't happen.

Becca's eyes shimmer with unshed tears when I finally look up at her again. "Oh sweetie. I never knew."

Even though my throat is clogged, I swallow and keep going. "Jack and I tried for the first five years. When kids didn't come along we just told ourselves that we didn't want them. We both avoided talking about it after a while." I shrug.

"No wonder you're so torn up," Rebecca says as she shakes her head in sympathy. "Dragging your feet isn't the answer. You're just delaying the inevitable. Max needs to know the truth. Either he'll be okay with not having kids or he'll walk away. But at least you won't be in limbo anymore."

I knew Becca would be honest with me and give me good advice. *Am I brave enough to take it?*

Chapter Twenty-Five

Max

As our relationship enters its third month, I decide that I need to figure out what Maddie wants. Maybe we're not on the same page. I turn onto her driveway, determined to have an honest talk.

When Maddie meets me at the door, I nearly change my mind. She's wearing tight black leggings and a long-sleeved black T-shirt. She looks like Catwoman and it takes my breath away. *Why rock the boat?*

"Something smells good!" The aroma hits me right as I cross the threshold.

"If I remember correctly, Mr. Connor, you said that you love beef stroganoff. So, that's what we're having!"

I pull her in for a quick kiss. She responds like she always does and the passion flares between us. When she draws back, she gives me a saucy smile and heads into the kitchen. I follow.

"Let Fibi in. He's chasing leaves in the backyard." Maddie says with laughter in her voice.

I look out the back door and sure enough the border collie is chasing leaves much like I expect he would herd sheep—with his complete focus and attention.

Pulling open the door, I shout, "Fibi, come in!"

The dog breaks his chase abruptly and skids to a stop. He reverses on a dime and runs into the house. I'm greeted with a cold nose as he presses his head into my hand. I pet him absently as I watch Maddie get dinner off the stove. Butterflies swarm in my stomach, not knowing if my upcoming questions are going to clear everything up between us or break everything apart.

"Go ahead and sit." She nods towards the table.

We settle into our chairs and fill our plates.

"Do you want some wine?"

I point to my glass already filled with ice water. "No, water's fine."

Her lips twitch.

"What?"

"You're not a wine guy, are you? If I offered beer, you wouldn't have turned that down."

I hold my hands up. "Busted!"

We both laugh. As I eat the delicious stroganoff, I look at the scene around me. We're in a cozy kitchen filled with homecooked aromas. A dog lies on his bed in the corner, perking up his head at our every word then lying back down. The woman of my dreams sits across from me looking sexy and sweet at the same time. *Do I really need more than this?*

It takes us no time to devour the salad, garlic bread, and the appetizing entrée. I wish we could dawdle more over the food, delaying the soul-searching conversation I need to have with Maddie. I should have paced myself better.

When Maddie hops up to the clear the table, I grab her hand and pull her into my lap. Our eyes lock. My heart rate doubles knowing what I'm going to say next. She looks at me quizzically, probably wondering why I pulled her into my lap if I'm not going to kiss her. I drag in a big breath.

"Maddie, I love you, and I want to build a future with you. But I don't know what you're looking for. Do you want to get married again and have kids?" The words spurt out of my mouth without finesse. I'm as surprised as she is with the bluntness of my question.

I feel her body go stiff for a beat or two. Then she winces and stands up.

"Well, that's not the reaction I was hoping for," I say in a bitter voice.

"It's not what you think." She glances up at the ceiling as if it holds the answer to my question.

I wait as emotions flash across her face. I see sadness and regret, then her eyes get a determined look. "There's something I need to tell you."

My heart sinks at her flat tone. It isn't encouraging. Have we been on a different page all these months?

She takes a big breath. "Max, I'm not sure that I can have children. You see, Jack and I tried several times without success. Watching you around Jamal and your excitement over Hailey and Quinn's baby has brought my biggest fear to the forefront. What if we can't have kids? How are you going to feel about that?"

I try to keep a neutral expression on my face, but my brows draw together. This was the last thing I expected her to say. After a few seconds I pinch my nose and shake my head, trying to contain the overpowering emotions flowing through my body.

Maddie watches as my inner struggle plays out before her eyes, yet she says nothing.

After what feels like minutes but is probably only seconds, I sigh. "Maddie, I don't know how I feel about that."

Tears fill her eyes. She says in a small voice, "So where do we go from here?"

I need to get away from her so I can think. Her heartbroken expression is killing me. My chairs scrapes noisily on the floor as I stand. "I need some time to think about us. What our future means after what you just told me."

Her face crumples and I think she's going to cry.

"I'm sorry," I say as I walk quickly from the room. The front door slams with far too much finality behind me.

Chapter Twenty-Six

Maddie

Double dating with Quinn and Hailey has become a Friday night staple. After my clash with Max last night, I wonder if we're still meeting them for tacos at our favorite Mexican joint.

Maybe he's had time to cool off and think things over. Avoiding the elephant sitting between us, I pretend everything's normal and send a text around noon to check in.

Maddie: Are we still on for tacos with Hailey and Quinn?

When there's no immediate response, I slump down on the sofa, staring off into space. *Did we break up last night and I missed it?*

I monitor for a response all afternoon. It doesn't seem like Max's style to give me the silent treatment. When my phone finally dings, I almost drop it in my excitement to pick it up.

Max: Yes, let's go. I'll pick you up.

Although his terse response doesn't make me feel much better, I'll have a chance to talk to him again and maybe we can span this divide that's developed between us.

Max arrives on time, as usual. He looks gorgeous in his long-sleeve gray Henley and jeans. But his eyes don't meet mine. There's no kiss at the door, nothing, not even a peck on the cheek.

I want to fall at his feet and beg for his forgiveness. But it's not really forgiveness I need—I need his acceptance of me possibly not being able to give him children. Internally I wail at the hand I've been dealt, yet outwardly I remain stoic. A blanket of detachment surrounds me, keeping me from feeling anything.

Fibi comes up and Max bends down to pet him, breaking the moment. This isn't the time to have a heart-to-heart discussion, so I grab my coat and we head out.

Los Amigos is busier than usual. Looks like every high school student is here to get tacos prior to the football game. We should have gone to a different restaurant.

Hailey and Quinn are already here, waiting in the packed entry. We join them in the crush of bodies crunched into the small space.

"Great to see you!" I greet Hailey with a warm hug. We can no longer tightly embrace due to her emerging baby bump, although she's not huge yet. Max surely doesn't need another reminder of the bombshell I dropped on him last night. I force myself to smile at my friend. "I miss seeing you in yoga class. How are you feeling?"

She rubs her belly. "The baby is starting to keep me up at night. It seems I have to wake up to pee every hour. Otherwise, everything is just peachy!"

I laugh. Glancing out of my eye, I see Max and Quinn deep in conversation. Do Hailey and Quinn notice there's something wrong between me and my boyfriend? He usually has his arm around me or is holding my hand. His frostiness comes through loud and clear as he stands a few feet away from me. I feel a chill in the room just from his presence.

"How long is the wait?" I turn back to Hailey since Max is going to ignore me. She pretends not to notice Max's cold shoulder, but I'm sure she does.

"Fifteen minutes, and that was about five minutes ago," she says with a sigh.

"Come on, let's take a seat at the bar so you can get off your feet. The guys are ignoring us anyway." I get Max's attention and point to the bar as Hailey and I walk over. He nods but doesn't move to join us.

After I help Hailey awkwardly climb into the tall bar stool, I join her. We order iced tea, much to the bartender's chagrin.

"Is something wrong with Max? He doesn't seem to be his energetic self." Hailey broaches the subject while sipping on her tea.

"I think he's working too much and he's getting burned out." I spout the first excuse that comes to mind. I like Hailey a lot but I don't think we're close enough to talk about this yet.

She nods. "We are super busy! I'm adding to his stress because he knows he needs to find another office manager in a few months. It's a lot, especially with the holidays approaching."

I shrug, knowing I can't spit out the truth, not until I've talked to Max first to see where we stand. Hailey and I sip our teas and discuss baby preparations, namely painting and getting the baby's room ready. They did the early genetic test and found out they're having a girl, so Hailey selected a light pink with white accents for the baby's room. It sounds adorable. A pang of hurt and regret slams my heart. I want to shout at the heavens. *Why can't I have kids?*

"Connor, party of four!" The hostess bellows out over the crowd noise.

Quinn comes over to help Hailey from her chair while Max follows the hostess alone to our table. When we join him, I give him a raised eyebrow and a frown, but he ignores me. Tonight's going to be a long night.

~*~

I hate every minute of the ride back to my house. Max and I sit in stony silence. Without our companions to keep up the conversation, we have nothing to say to each other.

Max walks me to the door and I'm not even sure he'll come in, but he does. We remove our coats and sit on the couch with a few feet between us. I grind my teeth in frustration.

Once inside, I can't keep my tongue in check any longer. "Tell me what you decided after last night's conversation." I surprise even myself at my boldness.

Max looks at his feet for several minutes. The long silence hangs around us like a fog and I start to sweat. *Is he breaking up with me?*

Finally, Max looks over at me. He isn't smiling. "Maddie, I want to get married and have kids with someone who loves me. After last night . . ." His declaration explodes between us like an atomic bomb. I feel the aftershocks as they hit my body.

Tears press hot against my eyes, and emotion clogs my throat. "So, where do we go from here?" I repeat my line from last night like a parrot. My voice cracks and I suck in my breath.

He turns fully towards me but doesn't touch me. "I think I need to take a break. Face it, our relationship is stalled. I know I want more . . . Marriage and a family . . ." He shrugs, then exhales deeply. "I don't know if we'll be *able* to move forward. Maddie, do you love me?" His eyes search mine as if he can find the answer in their depths.

My heart screams at me to say *Yes, of course I do*, but my head tells me it isn't fair to ask him to give up his dream of having children. I bite my lips while a few tears escape. Max raises his hand as if he wants to wipe them away but then drops it back in his lap. Even though we're sitting only a few feet apart, it feels like there's a chasm between us.

"Let's give it a few weeks so we can each think about what we want." He stands and looks at me still sitting on the couch. "The future of our relationship is frustrating and confusing. I'm sorry Maddie."

Max grabs his coat from the rack by the door and rushes out. The loud click of the door latch sounds like a gunshot in the room.

I sit in shock for several minutes, tears streaming unchecked down my face. Fibi finally wanders over and licks my hand.

Have I lost Max forever?

Chapter Twenty-Seven

Max

Breaking up with Maddie was one of the hardest things I've ever done. But we can't keep going on as we are. Stuck in one place and never moving forward.

After I thought about it a bit, the confession about whether she can have kids didn't surprise me. In the back of my mind I always wondered why Jack and Maddie never had children—especially since they were married for seven years and by all indications she likes kids. Seeing her interact with Jamal at the Twins game made me imagine Maddie and me sitting at a game with two rambunctious kiddos of our own. Sure, there are other ways to bring children into our life—adoption, mentoring more kids, or just being the best aunt and uncle to my siblings' offspring. To be honest though, I haven't yet reconciled if I don't want children of my own.

What really gets me is: Why didn't she express these concerns to me earlier? The frustration of having to decide something that monumental makes me want to give up on Maddie and me. What future do we have, and is it one I can accept?

And then the biggest thing of all. I told her I love her and she said nothing back. I was sure she was falling in love with me as much as I was with her. But maybe I was just deluding myself.

"Hey, boss. The shingles were just delivered. Are you ready to start putting them on?" My construction foreman Luke pulls me abruptly from my gloomy thoughts.

I look at him and nod. We're completing construction on a roomy two-story for a family of four. Watching this happy, loving family makes my heart hurt. I thought one day Maddie and I would be raising two kids and moving into a new Connor Construction house. Now that doesn't seem even remotely possible.

"Sure, let's go put that roof on," I say with as much enthusiasm as I can muster, which isn't much. Luke shakes his head and leaves me to collect my tools and join him.

~*~

We've been working for over an hour. My crew and I work together like a well-oiled machine after years of practice. Tom and Shorty pass Luke and I shingles and we nail them in place. The pounding of our nail guns echoes throughout the neighborhood. The air is cold, but I barely notice as I work up a sweat doing manual labor.

I hoped the task would get Maddie out of my mind, but it doesn't.

"Let's take five," I say. Tom throws me a water bottle and we rest while drinking our cool beverages.

"The shingles are looking good! We should have this job done by tomorrow as long as it doesn't rain or snow," Luke says conversationally.

Tom and Shorty voice their agreement while I remain silent.

"Cat got your tongue boss?" Shorty says. My crew have been avoiding me since I broke up with Maddie. I guess my grumpiness is not going unnoticed. I can't seem to drag myself out of this funk.

I grunt and drink the rest of the water in my bottle. Luke, Tom, and Shorty all exchange a look but don't challenge my silence.

I'm not in the mood for small talk.

"Okay guys let's get back to work," I say. My brain needs to focus on this job and quit fretting over Maddie.

The guys scramble to get back into position. I set a rapid pace in order to drive myself into physical exhaustion.

As we work our way up the roof, the steep pitch makes it more difficult to work quickly, but I don't slow down. Usually I'm the one most focused on safety, yet today I don't care a thing about it. My crew's safety—yes. My own—no.

146

"Max, aren't you working a little too close to the edge? Put on a safety rope before you go any further," Luke says.

I glare over at him. "I'm fine. Keep working."

My reckless response surprises my men by the looks on their faces, but none of them challenge me. They silently try to keep up my pace.

Tom throws a shingle at me which isn't quite on target, but I manage to catch it. His tosses have become less accurate as he tires beside me, but I ignore his and my fatigue and the fact that we should take a break or quit. I can't stop or I'll fall apart over the breakup.

I'm almost at the peak and very near the side of the roof when one of Tom's throws makes me stretch out to make the catch. Right as I'm grabbing for the shingle, I lose my balance. My feet slip out from under me and I slide precariously down the roof, trying to grab anything I can hold on to. Luke shouts something but I don't understand him.

Without something to grab, I gain momentum, slide to the edge and fall off the roof. Everything moves in slow motion as I feel myself free falling towards the ground. My brain tells me to try to break my fall with my arms, so I extend them out. Time slows and I notice every blade of grass as the yard rushes up to meet me.

The impact with the earth is even more jarring than expected. I slam into the grass and come to an abrupt stop, tumbling over onto my back. Time, that was moving so quickly before, now stands still, making my agony more acute. It's as if I'm being stabbed by hundreds of knives in a slow torture. Pain rushes up my shoulder and arm. I lay motionless for several seconds, trying to catch the breath that was forced from my lungs.

"Max, are you okay?" The urgency in Luke's voice penetrates the fog I'm in. I gasp for breath and shake my head, trying to clear it, but the ache in my shoulder is overwhelming. It's too painful to move. Eventually I'm able to breathe again, after several seconds of acting like a fish out of water and gasping for air.

Luke, Tom, and Shorty surround me with anxious looks on their faces. I hear Shorty calling 9-1-1 and asking for an ambulance. They don't move me—probably afraid I've broken my neck.

"My shoulder hurts, but I can move my arms and legs," I finally croak out, demonstrating moving those limbs.

"Lie still, boss. Help is on the way," Tom says as he kneels beside me, putting a firm hand on my shoulder.

After a few minutes, I mutter, "So much for finishing the roof today."

Tom and Shorty utter a relieved laugh at my attempted humor. Luke scowls at me. He knows as well as I do that it's my fault for ignoring safety procedures. With me banged up, my team is going to be one man down for quite some time. I mentally berate myself for being stupid and selfish.

A siren sounds in the distance. Once the ambulance arrives, things happen quickly. They put me on a stretcher and I grimace at the pain, breathing deeply through my nose to keep from passing out. Two paramedics load me into the vehicle, one staying in back with me, the other running to the front to drive.

As the remaining paramedic locks my stretcher in place, I shout to Luke, "Let Hailey know that I'm headed to the hospital." The EMT is strapping himself in and reaches for the door. "And have her tell Maddie!" I add in a rush. Luke nods right before the door slams. The siren screams as we rush away.

Chapter Twenty-Eight

Maddie

I'm preparing for my afternoon calculus class when my cell phone starts dancing across my desk. Turning it over, I see Hailey's smiling face.

"Hailey, what's up?" I answer with a grin. She and I have been meeting regularly for lunch despite my breakup with Max. I assume she's calling to tell me what's she's hungry for today.

There's a brief pause, then Hailey says, "Maddie, Max has been in an accident. They're taking him to the hospital right now."

My heart stops. The word accident smashes my peaceful world, bringing back all the horrific memories of the day Jack died. The smile falls from my face. My hands start to shake.

"Is he okay?" The lump in my throat almost blocks my ability to speak. My words come out as a whisper.

"He fell off the roof and they think he broke something. We won't know all the details until the doctor sees him." She pauses, then continues. "He's injured, but he's going to recover. I know this must be a terrible reminder . . ." Her voice trails off.

I take several calming breaths. *He's not dead. He's not dead* . . . Like a mantra, I remind myself over and over that this is different than what happened to Jack. Everything's going to be alright.

"He asked for us to tell you. I don't know where things are exactly between you, but I think you should go see him. Do you want me to come get you? Are you okay to drive?" my sweet friend offers.

Somewhere in the back of my mind a small burst of relief wars with the dread I'm still fighting down. He asked for me. That has to be a good sign, right? I nod, then remember she can't see me. "Yes, I'm okay. I'll leave as soon as I can get someone to cover my class."

"If you need anything, let me know. Quinn is already on his way to the hospital. I'm staying at the office for now."

Tears start streaming down my face. "Thank you, Hailey. I'll get there as soon as I can."

I hesitate to call William to ask him to cover my class since he's been rather frosty after our dating disaster. But my need to get to Max overcomes my aversion to ask Professor Bolton for help. Once William answers, my words come out in spurts. The emotion in my voice is evident by how many times I stop in order not to sob uncontrollably on the phone.

William finally cuts me off after my third attempt not to cry. "Maddie, go get your guy. I can tell you love him," he says.

His kind words make the waterworks even worse, but I manage to blubber, "Thank you."

"Go on, your Calc 101 students are safe with me."

I grab my purse and run to my car. The fear rushing through my body is almost overwhelming. William's words finally sink in and they hit me like a blow to the chest—I love Max with all my heart. Hopefully it's not too late to tell him.

~*~

I rush into the emergency room, frantically looking to see who to talk to about Max. Quinn is pacing on the other side of the room, and I run over to him and grab his arm. He envelopes me in a bear hug and I start sobbing into his chest. We stand there for minutes as I cry uncontrollably.

"He's going to be okay, Maddie. They think it's just a dislocated shoulder. We should be able to see him soon," Quinn says, rubbing my back.

I pull away, wiping my runny nose on my hand. "I'm sorry for being such a mess," I say as I point towards Quinn's damp shirt.

He smiles. "You love him, don't you?"

Nodding furiously, I say, "Yes, with all my heart. I need to tell him as soon as we can see him!"

Quinn nods. "You go in first, Maddie. What you have to tell him is more important than the teasing I'm going to give him about falling off a roof."

A small laugh escape my lips and I give Quinn a tearful smile.

A man clad in blue scrubs walks into the waiting room. "Who's here to see Max Connor?"

Quinn and I run over to him, both saying, "We are!"

"I'm Dr. Chen," the man says to me, holding out a hand, which I shake. "Mr. Connor suffered a separated shoulder and broken arm, but he's going to be fine. He just needs to take it slow for several weeks. Complete bed rest for the first week." He pauses and nods at Quinn as if they know each other. Referring to a chart in his hand, he continues, "We've given him some medicine for pain, so he might be a little groggy. Which one of you wants to see him first?"

Quinn pushes me forward. I follow the doctor down the hallway. The smells of antiseptic assault my nose. Dr. Chen's shoes squeak noisily on the tile floor.

The doctor motions for me to enter the room marked 211. I push open the door and enter. My heart pounds in my chest and my hands shake. I approach the bed where Max lies still. I wonder if he's sleeping.

I stand for a few minutes, gazing at him and thanking God that he's alive. Then, I take his hand and squeeze. His eyes flutter open and he stares at me. I smile when he squeezes my hand slightly in return.

His left shoulder is in a sling and his arm in a cast. They have his shoulder sling strapped to his chest, keeping that side of his body motionless. He looks a little pale in the white hospital gown. I want to kiss him until he's blushing like a tomato and neither of us can breathe.

"You gave me quite a scare, Mr. Connor!" My voice is shaky, but I grasp his hand tightly. When he firmly squeezes back my heart soars, knowing that he's able to move his hand and that he's possibly even happy to see me.

He smiles but remains silent. That's okay with me, because I need to say what's on my mind now that I have his undivided attention.

I perch on the side of the bed, still holding his hand. A few more tears flow down my cheeks. Taking a big breath, my words tumble from my lips. "Max, this accident scared me to death, but it also made me realize that I can't live without you. I've been miserable for the last few weeks . . ." He looks like he's going to say something, but I put my finger to his lips, cutting off his words.

"I've waited too long to tell you that I. Love. *You.*" I say the words passionately so he doesn't have any doubts about whether I mean them.

Max's eyes shimmer with tears. "I love you, too."

I nod, then rush on to address the remaining issue head-on, "What about having kids? I want to make sure we talk about this, rather than sweeping it under the rug. If you can accept that I may not be able to have children, then I'm all yours."

We now both have tears leaking from our eyes. *Wish I had a tissue.*

Max clears his throat, "Did you and Jack ever get tested to see why you weren't able to conceive?"

I look down, a little embarrassed to admit this next part. "No, we didn't."

He puts his finger under my chin and tilts my head back up. "Let's give it a few months of trying and if we can't get pregnant, we'll go to as many specialists as we can!"

I blush at his words while at the same time my hearts soars with the possibilities. Me, Max, marriage *and children.*

"What do you say Maddie?"

The quiet words spurs me on and I realize that I need to be the one to say it. Lay my cards out on the table. Max told me that I needed to make the next move. It wasn't a simple "I love you" that he was looking for, it was a commitment. A vow to move on and build a life with him. To face the issue of fertility together. I've been such a fool!

Leaning closer I kiss him slowly and with passion. I want him to have no doubt about how I feel, but I need to say it in words and not just actions. Looking into his beautiful blue eyes, I say, "Max Connor will you marry me? The sooner the better!"

I feel him chuckle and he squeezes my hand again. "Yes, Maddie, I'll marry you."

I whoop an excited yell and throw my arms around Max's neck, careful to avoid his injured shoulder. We kiss for several seconds until I hear someone clear their voice. Turning, I see Dr. Chen hovering at the door.

"Do you Connors all get engaged at the hospital?" he asks with a big smile on his face.

We laugh, then Max whispers in my ear, "We're getting married as soon as possible." I smile and nod in agreement. We've waited too long already.

Chapter Twenty-Nine

Max

"You're the worst patient ever, Maxwell Connor! Get back in that bed!" Maddie glares at me with her hands on her hips. This is my third jailbreak attempt this morning, but none of them have worked. The professor's guest bedroom has become my jail cell, yet I wouldn't want to be anywhere else.

I grumble and climb back under the covers. My warden fluffs the pillows behind my back. I pull her into a sloppy kiss, which she participates in for a few seconds, then pulls away.

"You're so cute when you're bossy," I say with a smirk. The diamond ring Quinn helped me procure sparkles brightly on her finger. Who knew my grand gesture, as Quinn calls it, was falling off a roof? Not very romantic, but very effective.

She gives me a stern expression, but I see a smile hovering behind her strict façade.

"You have a visitor. I'll bring him in."

I hear voices in the hall, and Maddie returns with Jacob trailing behind her. He walks in and sits in the visitor's chair positioned beside the bed. He's the only Connor who hasn't visited me so far. But what is he doing here on a Tuesday at 10:30 in the morning?

Maddie smiles at him, obviously pleased that he's made the effort to visit. "Do you guys need anything?"

I look at my brother and he shakes his head. "We're good," I say.

My fiancée smiles and disappears.

"I'm surprised you're here on a weekday. What's up?"

My brother frowns, then clears his throat. "I was laid off yesterday, so I'm visiting for a while. I'm staying with Mom and Dad."

My mouth hangs open. Jacob worked for an advertising firm in Minneapolis, but by all accounts, everything was going well other than all the overtime they expected.

"I'm sorry to hear that. Are you going to look for another job in Minneapolis?"

He shakes his head. "Not right away. I need a breather. Plus, I know a certain construction crew that's down a man and could use my help." He smiles.

I sit up straighter. "Great idea! We can really use your help! I'll call Luke and see where he can use you. When do you want to start?" I can't hide the excitement in my voice that my little brother is back home. Maybe we can convince him to stay like we convinced Quinn.

"How about tomorrow?"

We shake hands, then high-five. As the reality of the situation sinks in, I have a thought. "Are you sure you can live with Mom? She'll try to arrange a date for you with every one of her friends' single daughters, ya know."

Jacob cringes. "Definitely a downside. But I don't know how long I'll be here, so an apartment is out of the question. I can't stay with Quinn and Hailey with the new baby coming. Staying with you at your girlfriend's house would be . . . just awkward." He raises an eyebrow.

I point to my shoulder sling and cast. "It's not like that. I'm incapacitated for a while."

"Right," he smirks.

"Well, at least you'll enjoy Mom's home cooking."

Nodding, my brother replies, "Except for Ash's healthy salads!"

A belly laughs escapes and I feel my shoulder twinge at the movement. I grimace at the pain.

A worried look crosses Jacob's face. "I should go. Maddie says you need your rest."

Rolling my eyes at what my overly protective warden told my brother, I capitulate. Just talking makes me tired nowadays. "I'll have Luke call you to let you know which jobsite he needs you at. Thanks for helping, Jacob. I'm glad you're home."

Jacob walks to the door and then turns. "Me too. Connor's Grove is a nice change from the big city."

I watch his retreating back. Funny how things work out.

~*~

"You have another visitor!" Maddie wakes me from my third nap this afternoon, excitement obvious in her voice.

"Who is it?" I grumble and open my eyes.

"Don't be such a grump," she says, then sticks her tongue out at me and disappears.

Craning my neck to peer down the hall, a small figure makes his way towards my room. I recognize his awkward gait and a smile splits my face. I swivel my eyes to look at the framed photo of our threesome at the Twins game that sits proudly on the nightstand.

Jamal enters the room with Fibi at his heels. "Mr. Connor, how are you doing?"

I chuckle. "When are you going to start calling me Max?"

He sits in the chair by my bed, feet dangling, swinging back and forth. Fibi sits just out of range of his feet.

Ignoring my comment, Jamal says, "Sorry to hear about your injury. Does it still hurt?" He eyes the sling holding my shoulder in place and the cast on my arm.

"Not really. But I have to be careful about how much I move around."

His small hand reaches over to pet the dog. "Miss Maddie says that Fibinoochi competes in Agility competitions. I'm gonna check out a book about that from the library!"

"Are you?" I act surprised even though I'm not.

He nods. "Miss Maddie invited me to come with you on his next competition! I'll make sure I've read the book first and can give her plenty of pointers."

I cough into my hand, trying to suppress my laughter.

"Oh, I almost forgot!" He reaches into his coat pocket pulling out a wrinkled envelope. "Mom said to give this to you."

Tearing open the yellow envelope, I pull out a bent *Get Well Soon* card. The inside of the card contains a series of knock-knock jokes. Jamal's illegible signature is scribbled at the bottom.

"Those are the funniest jokes I've ever heard. Thought it would make you feel better."

"Why don't you read me a few and I'll try to guess." I hand the card back to him.

Giggling, he says, "Knock knock."

Obviously, the next part is easy. "Who's there?" I reply.

"Gorilla."

"Gorilla who?"

"Gorilla me a hamburger!" He almost falls out of the chair with laughter. I grin.

Fibi looks on, raising one of his ears and tilting his head.

"Okay, I'll do one more!"

I nod.

"Knock knock."

"Who's there?"

"Police," he giggles again.

"Police who?"

"Police stop telling these awful knock-knock jokes." The kid bends over, holding his stomach and laughing.

Maddie enters. "What's all the laughing about?"

Jamal straightens up and exchanges a look with me, suddenly serious.

"Guy talk," I reply.

"Yep. Guy talk," Jamal repeats, solemnly nodding.

She rolls her eyes. "How about I bring in some cookies? Is anyone hungry?"

Jamal shoots to his feet. "I am!" He thrusts the card back into my hand, joining Maddie in the doorway.

"Okay, you can help me carry the snacks." She ruffles Jamal's curly black hair affectionately and gives me a wink. One way or another, we will always have children in our life.

Chapter Thirty

Maddie

The drive is shorter than I remember. I haven't been here in a couple of months.

My feet crunch on the frozen ground as I walk towards my destination. The overcast sky adds an air of gloom. I picked the spot near the big oak tree because Jack loved the outdoors. The tree provides shade in the summer and turns a breathtaking shade of red in the fall. Right now, it stands like a silent sentry with its arms stretched towards the heavens.

Kneeling, I ignore the cold biting through my blue jeans. My fingers trace his name on the black granite stone. A tear trickles down my cheek.

"Jack," my voice cracks and I bite my lip. I take a few more minutes to collect myself. "I'm getting married in a few weeks. His name is Max Connor."

I nod as if I'm having a conversation with him. "Yes, his great-grandparents founded Connor's Grove. I guess you would say that I'm marrying into town royalty." A small laugh escapes my lips.

Is this a bad idea? Asking my dead husband for his blessing?

I continue talking to the headstone. "You see, I wanted you to know how much I loved you, but Max has found a place in my heart . . . I love him, Jack. Very much."

Tears roll unchecked down my cheeks. I blink furiously, trying to stem the flow, but it doesn't help. I swipe them away with my coat sleeve, then finish what I came here to say. "He's a wonderful man. He made me see everything I've been missing now that you're gone . . . Fibi and I even started competing again because of him. Max loves me for being me—the nerdy math whiz. Just like you did, Jack."

A strong wind kicks up from the west. I pull the hood of my coat up to shield me from the bitter cold. Standing, I rub the top of the stone, the smooth, solid surface unyielding under my fingertips. Not ready to leave yet, I loiter for several beats, looking across the barren cornfields surrounding this peaceful place. The lump in my throat makes it difficult to swallow. I pull in a few deep breaths.

"I'll still come visit, and maybe one day bring Max and our kids with me." My voice cracks on the words *kids*, but my sweet fiancé has given me hope that maybe we can have some.

As I turn to leave, the gray clouds part and the sun peeks through, spreading warmth and sunshine across the barren landscape. Blue sky is visible for the first time in over a week. I tilt my head towards the sun and bask in the warmth for several minutes. My tears dry on my cheeks.

I smile, turning back to look at the headstone one more time. Jack is giving me his blessing by blowing away my guilt and warming my heart with sunshine. A part of me will always love Jack, but he won't intrude anymore. He's a fond memory now.

I walk back to my car with a joyful heart.

~*~

The bridal salon is hopping, but I spot my companions immediately. Since I was out and about, I agreed to drop by for my last fitting before the wedding. I thought that my previous errand would ruin trying on my wedding dress again, but instead it gives me a spring in my step and a smile on my face. I can live in the present now.

"Maddie!" Ash, Hailey, and Becca surround me with hugs and laughter. "We can't wait to see you in your dress," they exclaim together.

"I can't wait to see Hailey in hers!" Turning, I say to Ash and Becca, "And I'm so glad that you two want to share my last fitting with me." Sniffles fill the air while Becca hands out tissues.

Because we're having such a small wedding, we're only having two attendants. Quinn is Max's best man and Hailey is my maid of honor.

A salesperson comes over, carrying two dresses enclosed in plastic. She smiles and guides us to the dressing rooms.

"Do you want my help getting into your dresses?" she asks Hailey and me.

"I could use some help," Hailey says with a giggle as she points to her protruding stomach.

The saleslady disappears with Hailey to the next dressing room.

"Ash and Becca, please help me with my dress," I say as I tug them into my dressing room.

The plastic crinkles when Ashleigh removes my dress from the bag. We all stare at the gorgeous creation. It's a simple off-the-shoulder design void of embellishments. No lace or glittery beads. The slinky white silk feels buttery soft to my fingers.

Once Ash slips the dress over my head and zips me up, I turn towards the mirror. The person staring back at me looks like a bride. I'm breathless for a second, knowing that the dress is perfect.

"You're beautiful Maddie! Max is going to faint when he sees you," Becca says with delight.

I laugh. "Hopefully not. I need him to get through the ceremony first!"

Hailey emerges in her knee-length blue dress. The color matches Max's eyes—just as I intended.

"Gorgeous!" Ash, Becca, and I exclaim together as we look at the beautiful pregnant lady.

Grabbing my sisters-in-laws' hands, I say, "Both Connor brothers are going to faint when they see us!"

Our laughter fills the salon.

Since the salesperson has disappeared, Ash goes with Hailey to assist her getting out of her dress. When Becca and I are alone back in my dressing room, I turn to her and grasp her hands.

"Becca, you will always be my sister-in-law. I hope you know that even though I'm moving on, I'll always have a place in my heart and my life for you. It took me awhile, but I finally realized that by letting Max and the Connors into my heart, I wasn't pushing out Jack and the Hendersons. My heart is big enough to fit all of you!"

She squeezes my hands and the sniffles return. I see tears in her eyes and her lips wobble. Taking a big breath, Becca replies, "Thank you for saying that. I'm so happy for you, and I'm glad that we can share you with the Connors. Jack would be happy for you too."

I smile and nod. *Yes, he already told me.*

Chapter Thirty-One

Max

"Do you want to wear a tux?"

Maddie's sitting in the guest chair, taking wedding notes on her laptop. We're getting married in two weeks at the chapel near my grandparent's farm. Mom's playing the role of wedding planner, which Maddie seems content with except for the fact that she keeps having to rein Mom in from going overboard. We both keep reminding her that we want a small, intimate wedding with less than 50. Mom wants to plan for 500. Maddie also requested that she be able to plan her own and my attire for the wedding.

"Do you want me to wear a tux?" I counter.

She stares at me over the computer, glasses perched on the end of her adorable nose. "I'm wearing a wedding dress, so I guess the answer is yes."

I smile with the vision of Maddie in a white wedding dress filling my mind. She's going to rock whatever dress she chooses.

Wedding details are starting to bore me, though, so I change the subject. "How about we sit on the back patio this afternoon? I'm going stir-crazy being inside all day."

My warden peers at me; the stern expression on her face tells me that my brilliant suggestion is not going to fly. "Dr. Chen said one full week of bedrest. I'm following his instructions to a T."

I frown, emitting a grumpy groan.

"Mr. Connor, you need to be fully recovered in two weeks! I want you to not have to wear that sling at our wedding or on our wedding night. Do you get my drift?" Maddie waggles her eyebrows at me, and I blush. Where has this Maddie been all this time?

She giggles, then comes over and sits beside me on the bed. "I suppose if you're careful we can sit outside this afternoon," she whispers in my ear, then kisses me on the neck.

I turn to kiss her fully on her mouth. Our kiss escalates, leaving me breathless. "You don't play fair, professor!"

"I know," she says, then primly returns to the chair, picks up her computer, and squints at the screen. "How do you feel about cummerbunds? We can get them to match Hailey's dress and my flowers."

Another groan escapes my lips and my fiancée looks at me. I try to project a charming smile. "Whatever you want, sweetheart. I just want to marry you as soon as possible." Plus, I'm not exactly sure what a cummerbund is although I won't admit it.

She smiles. "A blue cummerbund it is. And I'm going to choose chocolate for the cake."

No surprise there. I smile back.

~*~

We're married on a windy Saturday in late October. Everyone has their fingers crossed that we don't have an early fall snowstorm during the wedding. So far, so good.

My heart swells when the professor walks down the aisle in the tiny chapel towards me. Gramps was chosen to give her away. A task that he's taking very seriously. Maddie's wearing a knee-length white dress that hugs her curves and takes my breath away. The off-the-shoulder design is sexy without being revealing. Her hair is up in a sophisticated bun, showing off her elegant neck. There's no veil to hide her gorgeous smile. I'm going to plant kisses all over those creamy shoulders and neck later tonight. I can't wait.

Quinn stands beside me in his matching black tux. Hailey is standing on the other side of the altar, looking pretty in her sky-blue dress. Maddie explained that the high waistline would help hide Hailey's pregnant belly although I'd say her pregnancy won't go without notice.

When my bride reaches me, I hold out my hand. She takes it and I pull her into position facing me. Her beauty and happy smile make my heart rate accelerate. I have to remind myself to breathe in slowly, then exhale. The pastor gives his prepared speech, but I don't hear a word.

Glancing across the crowd in the intimate chapel, I see the Connors lining the entire front row. Jamal, his grandmother, and his mom are sitting in the second row along with my construction crew. Amber, Doug, Gloria, and Charlie Robinson—along with a squirming Noah—reside in the third row. Jim and Rebecca Henderson smile broadly from the next row. Logan sits next to Jim while baby Ella is perched on Becca's lap. A sprinkling of other friends round out the crowd. Maddie's sweet, but firm, tactics kept the guest list below fifty, even though Mom proposed additional attendees up until just one week ago.

"Do you take this woman to be your wife . . ." Pastor Ron asks, and I focus back on my bride. My heart skips a beat when I put the ring on her finger. A tear rolls down her face when she puts my ring on my finger, and I gently wipe it away with my thumb. She whispers, "They're happy tears because I love you so much." We gaze at each other, my eyes reflecting how much I love her as well.

"You may now kiss the bride." The words I've been waiting for! Without any hesitation, I pull Maddie into an embrace and kiss her until she's breathless. "Just wait for tonight," I whisper in her ear and she turns beet red at my promise. Fortunately, I ditched the sling last week, giving me full use of both my arms.

When we turn towards the crowd, they jump to their feet and cheer. Maddie holds her bouquet over her head as if she just won a prize. We walk down the aisle while family and friends clap and smile. Jamal fist pumps and high-fives me when we walk by.

Everyone's invited to the wedding reception to be held at my grandparents' farmhouse. It's large enough to hold all our guests comfortably. Mom and Nana have been cooking all week, and I can't wait to sample the delicious food. Mom was in her element planning and taking care of all the details for this wedding. Maddie even mentioned that Mom should become a professional wedding planner.

We stop when we reach the back of the sanctuary and I pull my wife into another tight embrace. "Are you happy, Mrs. Connor?"

She smiles up at me. "I'm happy to infinity and back!"

What else did I expect from a math professor?

Epilogue

Maddie

I'm bubbling with anxious energy as we sit in the waiting room at my doctor's office. My husband holds my hand and we stare at each other with sappy smiles on our faces. I just found out I'm pregnant a few weeks ago and I'm having an ultrasound to check on everything. We told the family last evening because I wanted to err on the side of caution and not say anything sooner. Max was ready to shout the news from the rooftop as soon as we found out. Needless to say, the family is overjoyed. Hailey was especially excited that soon-to-arrive baby Lilly will have a cousin to play with.

"Why are you nervous?" my husband asks as I continue to jiggle my leg.

I put my hand on my leg to stop the motion. "I'm excited. Maybe she'll be able to tell the baby's sex."

Max gives me a funny look. "Are you sure you don't want it to be a surprise?"

I frown. "Why? Do you want it to be a surprise?"

He laughs. "Just pulling your chain professor. I know you're anxious to know if we're having a boy or a girl!"

"Mrs. Connor," a nurse in green scrubs with yellow smiley faces on them calls my name. We follow her into the exam room where she drills me with questions. "How's the nausea doing? Has vomiting been a problem?"

"Thankfully I made it through without vomiting! I think the nausea is just about done, too."

A small smile crosses her face while she types furiously on her laptop.

"How about constipation?"

When she glances up, I cringe, shaking my head. Out of the corner of my eye I see my husband blushing while the nurse continues typing.

"Have you noticed more heartburn or gas than usual?"

The neck of my shirt suddenly feels constricting. How many more of these embarrassing questions does she have?

"Um, no, I don't think so."

After several more clicks on her keyboard, she nods. "That's all for now. I'll give you a pamphlet with some possible second-trimester health complications and how to treat them."

The corners of my mouth quirk up. *I can't wait to read that.*

Once the interrogation is over, the nurse helps me onto the exam table. The stirrups stare back at me like a torture chamber device. At least she doesn't insist that I put my feet in them yet.

Once she leaves, Max shakes his head and says, "I'm sure glad I'm not a woman."

I chuckle. Wait until I go into labor.

Doctor Brant arrives and settles me back, putting some gel on the wand and turning on the ultrasound machine. The stirrups really aren't so bad. The doctor spends a few seconds sliding the probe around. A loud, rhythmic swooshing noise fills the room. Max grasps my hand tightly.

"That's your baby's heartbeat."

We all listen to the joyous sound for a few moments.

The doctor continues moving the wand around and peers closer to the screen.

"Can you tell the baby's sex?" I ask with excitement in my voice.

Doctor Brant looks up as she fiddles with the controls on the machine. "It's a little too soon to determine the sex."

My new mom excitement takes a little hit knowing that I'm going to have to wait a while to know whether we're having a boy or a girl.

The doctor takes another look at the screen and then turns to Max and I. The smile on her face tells me it's not bad news, but I still hold my breath.

"There's two heartbeats. Looks like you're having twins! Congratulations!"

"Really?" I squeal.

"I've got bionic swimmers!" Max declares.

The doctor laughs at him while I shake my head. He's so proud of his accomplishment at getting me pregnant so quickly that I'm never going to hear the end of it.

My husband embraces me, and we hug, laugh, and cry all at the same time. After all of my worries, this news blows me away. Two babies. We are truly blessed.

The doctor hands me a tissue and I loudly blow my nose. She brings Max and I back to reality when she says, "We need to watch your pregnancy closely, Mrs. Connor, due to your age and a first-time pregnancy, plus the fact that you're having twins. Be prepared to go on bed rest during your last month."

That throws a little cold water on our celebration, but Max whispers in my ear, "It's payback time, my dear. I'll be the warden this round and I can't wait."

I smack him in the arm, remembering what a terrible patient he was and how I had to keep him in line. *Maybe I shouldn't have been so strict.*

"We'll check again on the babies' sex at a future appointment when you're a little further along. Get dressed, and I'll see you for a few minutes in my office." The doctor closes the door behind her with a soft click.

Max and I stare at each other as we absorb the news.

"We need a bigger nursery," I say.

"We need a bigger house sooner rather than later," Max says, referring to my two-bedroom house that we've been occupying since the wedding. Max was going to build us a new one next spring. Even after clearing out all of Jack's things, there's still reminders of him, so we decided that it's time to move on. Literally.

"Get the blueprints drawn up and let's start making some decisions. Connor Construction needs to add us to their calendar."

My husband ponders my words, knowing that his small company is already stretched to the seams. "I need to hire another crew . . . Maybe Jacob will stay on long term . . ."

Putting my fingers to his lips, I cut off any further ruminations. "Shh. We'll make everything work. Don't look so worried."

He nods. "Right. We might be a little cramped for a while, but we have a roof over our heads. And two babies to love!" A grin splits his handsome face.

"I can't wait to meet them!" I say as I nod towards my stomach.

Max kisses me then rubs the barely noticeable baby bump. "Me either. One of them is probably going to be a physics professor and the other a math professor," he says with an exaggerated sigh.

Our laughter fills the room. Love fills my heart.

THE END

Note to Readers

Dear Reader—thank you for reading the second book in my Connor Brothers series. If you like small town romances and Hallmark movies, you'll love this series of clean and wholesome romances.

I hope Maddie and Max's story brought you many hours of happiness, some laughs, and maybe a few tears. While Connor's Grove is a fictitious community, there are small towns all over America where neighbors care about each other and help when times are tough.

I have fond memories of living in Minnesota for fifteen years. Hopefully I captured some things that make Minnesotans special—county–fair-winning brownies, planting a garden and the overflow of zucchini that you can hardly give away, the Minnesota accent (sentence ending eh's), and the loyalty that Twins and Vikings fans have for their teams—just to name a few. I threw in the exuberant matchmakers just for fun.

Jacob and Daisy's story (Book 3 in the Connor Brothers series) is coming Summer 2020. Please follow me on my website, Facebook, or Amazon author page or subscribe to my newsletter to be informed about upcoming book releases. Links to all of those are included in the "About the Author" chapter below.

Thank You and Happy Reading!

Acknowledgements

Thank you to my amazing editor Bonnie McKnight. Her suggestions and encouraging comments made this a much better story. She insisted that we put all the events on a timeline that was realistic and made sense. No one has a baby in 11 months! *Oops*.

I'm thankful for all the wonderful people in my life. A little piece of each of you finds its way into my stories. And I'm especially grateful to my supportive husband who chuckles when he sees himself in one of my books. He loves cherry pie. *Wink. Wink.*

About the Author

Leah Busboom wanted to become an author since the day she learned how to read! She specializes in the Romance genre because she loves a sweet love story with a happy ending. Her books are known for their heartwarming tales, intriguing characters, and hilarious real-life situations that will make you want to laugh out loud.

Leah currently lives in Colorado with her wonderful husband, her "Blue Bomber" bicycle, and a hundred bunny rabbits that roam free in the neighborhood.

Find out about Leah's latest book releases, sales, and giveaways!

- AuthorLeahBusboom.com
- Newsletter Sign-up
- Leah Busboom Facebook Author Page
- Amazon Author Page

Books by Leah Busboom:

Chance on Love Series Trilogy: (all available on Amazon.com)

- *Second Chances*—Matt and Samantha's story (Book 1)
- *Taking Chances*—Danny and Paige's story (Book 2) (Winner: 2018 Rocky Mountain Cover Art Contest— Sweetest Cover)
- *Lasting Chances*—Gabe and Megan's story (Book 3)
- Chance on Love Series Boxed Set – Books 1-3 in Chance on Love series

Unlikely Catches Series Trilogy:

- *Catching Cash's Heart*—Holly and Cash's story (Angel Wings & Fastballs) (Book 1) (One of **The 50 Best Indie Books of 2019**)
- *Stealing Alan's Heart*—Brianna and Alan's story (Stilettos & Spreadsheets) (Book 2)
- *Winning Trey's Heart*—Abby and Trey's story (Playboy & the Bookworm) (Book 3)
- *Unwrapping Sam's Heart* – Lynn and Sam's story (A Christmas Novella) (Prequel to Book 1)
- *Melting Nick's Heart* – Bethany and Nick's story (A Valentine's Day Novella) (Sequel to Book 3)

Connor Brothers Series:

- Finding You – Quinn and Hailey's story (Book 1)
- Loving You – Max & Maddie's story (Book 2)

Made in United States
Orlando, FL
22 July 2023

35381235R00096